Seven Stories
by James Hall

A SELECTION WITH AN INTRODUCTION

by

MARY BURTSCHI

FAYETTE COUNTY BICENTENNIAL
OF THE AMERICAN REVOLUTION COMMISSION
VANDALIA, ILLINOIS

Publication of this book has been made possible through grants from the Fayette County Board of Supervisors and the Illinois Bicentennial Commission. Additional financial assistance came from the City Councils of St. Elmo, Vandalia, Brownstown, Ramsey, and St. Peter.

Library of Congress Card No. 75-23549
Printed in the United States of America, 1975

ISBN 0-9601642-1-9

A FAYETTE COUNTY BICENTENNIAL OF THE AMERICAN REVOLUTION COMMISSION BOOK

To celebrate the nation's two hundredth birthday anniversary the Fayette County Board of Supervisors by a resolution formed the Fayette County Bicentennial of the American Revolution Commission. The county, organized in February, 1821, was named for Marquis de Lafayette, the French nobleman who joined General Washington's army in the American Revolution. Lafayette helped the Americans to defeat the besieged troops at Yorktown and was present at Cornwallis's surrender.

Historically, Lafayette is associated with the county that bears his name. In 1824 President Monroe invited him to come to the United States as the guest of this nation whose freedom he had helped to gain. Lafayette returned to America in August and in the spring of 1825 visited Illinois. Judge James Hall, who became a resident of Vandalia two years later, had the honor of delivering the address of welcome to General Lafayette when he arrived at Shawneetown on May 7, 1825. As the son of a Revolutionary soldier, Hall spoke with earnest appreciation. In one passage he said, "We enjoy the fruits of your courage, the lessons of your example. We are the descendants of those who fought by your side—we have imbibed their love of freedom—we inherit their affection for *La Fayette*."

James William Berry, the first talented artist of Illinois, served as the circuit clerk of Fayette County from 1826 to 1856. In 1839 he was commissioned by the Illinois General Assembly to copy Ary Scheffer's full-length Lafayette portrait, which has hung in the United States House of Representatives since 1825. James Hall's belongings included an engraving of Lafayette in the uniform of an American general. The likeness of the soldier brings to mind one writer's remark, "Marquis de Lafayette's French heart beat proudly under his American uniform."

Even today Fayette Countians remember Lafayette by tangible reminders of the past—Judge Hall's address of welcome, the engraving of the general which remains in Fayette County, and the Berry portrait which now hangs in the old state capitol at Springfield. The Fayette

County Bicentennial of the American Revolution Commission received a matching grant from the Illinois Bicentennial Commission to publish this book.

The membership of this County Commission includes Mrs. Eugene Grandfield, Brownstown; Mrs. Gene Denton, vice-chairperson, and Mrs. Howard Franklin, treasurer, Ramsey; Mrs. Revis Calvert, secretary, and Mrs. Neta Muma, St. Elmo; Miss Josephine Burtschi, Miss Mary Burtschi, chairperson, Mrs. Philip Cocagne, publicity chairperson, Mrs. Dale Tedrick, and Mr. Harry Truitt, Vandalia.

CONTENTS

Preface	7
Introduction	9
The French Village	20
The Indian Hater	34
Pete Featherton	47
A Legend of Carondelet	62
Michel de Coucy	75
The Silver Mine	89
The Seventh Son	99

PREFACE

A young man travelling down the Ohio River in 1820 in search of fame and fortune found it necessary to do many things before he could establish himself. Even with a natural bent toward literature, he was sometimes obliged to try farming or trade, and he certainly found it convenient if he could claim competence in one of the professions—medicine, law, or the ministry. But James Hall, freshly out of the army, was more versatile than most newcomers. He had been a soldier and a student of law; he would become an editor, a district attorney, a circuit judge, the state treasurer of Illinois, a banker, and always a writer of both verse and prose. This versatility extended even into the field of literature since he published biography, history, editorials, essays, short stories, one novel, and much incidental poetry. In his literary work he put to good use his varied experiences during a dozen years in Illinois and drew extensively on his observations of the burgeoning West. He had an eye for landscape and an ear for speech when he was not handicapped by the conventions of the age. In his best creative writing, his short stories, these traits are clearly manifest.

All of James Hall's work was published prior to the Civil War; today unfortunately his works are out of print. Anthologists, to be sure, have plucked an occasional tale from his books so that contemporary readers can become familiar with his sketches of life in the old French villages or his humorous treatment of worthies like Pete Featherton. And his story "The Indian Hater" has won fortuitous fame because of Herman Melville's inclusion of its salient details in his novel *The Confidence Man*. But there has been no modern edition of Hall's fiction.

The seven stories that Mary Burtschi has selected here to represent Hall are characteristic of the writer and reveal him at his aesthetic best. Miss Burtschi is well qualified to make this selection and to introduce Hall to a current audience. A native of Fayette County, Illinois, and an enthusiastic student of early Vandalia history, she has been able to rely on her extensive knowledge of the region in order to delineate Hall as a man of affairs as well as a writer. James Hall was an inveterately busy man during his twelve years in the infant state of Illinois. One may indeed wonder how with his burden of civic and political duties he found the time to write at all. Miss Burtschi's introduction is a sincere tribute to a man whose reputation has suffered unjustly since his death in Cincinnati over a century ago.

John T. Flanagan

INTRODUCTION

James Hall was born at Philadelphia in 1793, the son of John Hall, a well-to-do landowner in Maryland. Some disagreement exists as to the date of James's birth. According to the church record and the Bible of his mother, Sarah Ewing Hall, the date July 29 is given. In his autobiographical sketch, however, Hall himself says that he was born on August 19. This date is also engraved on his tombstone. To his mother, a member of an intellectual Philadelphia family, James owed a lasting interest in both reading and creative writing. In fact, Sarah Ewing Hall contributed to magazines and published literary conversations about the Bible.

Within six years after their marriage John and Sarah Hall moved from the ancestral estate in Maryland to Philadelphia. In the family library James read the classics which later formed his literary style. Likewise, the early nineteenth century attitudes and customs formed his mind and character. In the home of his grandfather John Ewing, the youth was exposed to literary, scientific, and political discussions. At the age of twelve he was sent to an academy near Philadelphia. Here he incurred the wrath of his teachers for his independent spirit and intense determination to think for himself.

In 1813 he enlisted in the Washington Guards, a Philadelphia corps of volunteers who guarded against landing parties from the British fleet on the Delaware River. Although James, like his brother John, held anti-war views, he must have felt that the British fleet had no right to raid farms and towns on the banks of the Delaware. In the army his friendship with Major Thomas Biddle helped to get him a commission as third lieutenant. Later Hall described memorably the battles of the War of 1812 in which he had fought.

Then in 1815 he served with a detachment of artillerymen on the naval expedition to Algiers. He kept a journal of the voyage in which he jotted down his observations of the Mediterranean scene. In a Byronic manner he recalled incidents of history as the vessel neared Cape Trafalgar or glided through the Strait of Gibraltar. One suspects that a copy of *Childe Harold's Pilgrimage* may have been tucked in his pocket.

In 1816 Hall remained in the army and elected the arsenal at Pittsburgh as his choice of posts. Here he turned to the legal profession.

He studied law under the direction of James Ross, his father's friend. Among Ross's distinguished and wealthy clients had been President Washington. Ross had served as a United States Senator from Pennsylvania during the years 1794–1803. After his withdrawal from politics, he was engaged in a profitable law practice in Pittsburgh. Indeed Hall must have admired his teacher very much. Among his belongings, after his death, was found an engraving of Ross made from a portrait painted by Thomas Sully. After Hall's admission to the bar in 1818, he became recognized as an able lawyer. Henry Eddy, a bright Pittsburgh youth, admired Hall's legal knowledge and decided to study law under his direction.

While residing in Pittsburgh, Hall also enjoyed its fashionable society. He received invitations to parties and dances from the wealthiest families. Dancing always excited his interest. Especially the feminine beauty and grace of his dancing partners pleased him. Upon his return home, he composed sentimental verses, exclusively devoted to them. Though romantic, the verses were marked by a lightness of touch and a pleasing sound. He sent them to his brother John, then the editor of the *Port Folio* of Philadelphia. Shortly after, they were published in the literary magazine.

Morgan Neville, the editor of the *Pittsburgh Gazette,* asked Hall to contribute arguments for the need of improved navigation facilities on the Ohio River. Henceforth Hall resolved to study this great river on which emigrants were moving westward. As he stared across the Ohio at the great expanse of trees, he contemplated a journey further on and a country little known to civilized man. At the same time, the picturesque frontiersmen, dressed in coonskin caps and deerskin clothes, coming in on the keelboats drew his attention and awakened speculations. Would a young lawyer have better opportunities moving westward? At any rate, he seriously pondered the idea of joining the settlers at a later time.

In April, 1820, he boarded a keelboat and journeyed down the Ohio in order to practice law in Illinois. The scenery would have induced any writer to pull a notebook from his pocket. Although no mountains dignify the scene, he commented, "Nature has worked with a rapid but masterly hand." Besides the landscape, he busily recorded descriptions of the various passengers, kinds of boats on the river, treatment of travelers, and river melodies. He also described places such as the thriving town of Pittsburgh and the Cumberland Road, that was being completed in "a manner which reflects the highest credit upon those engaged in its construction."

At Shawneetown, Illinois, where he landed, his eyes were fastened on the motley crowd of people. His mode of dress suddenly struck him as different. Perhaps he would buy a "get-up" more in keeping with his new surroundings. Within due time, however, he found other lawyers dressed as gentlemen. He was happy to see his friend Henry Eddy, who for the last two years had resided at Shawneetown. And within a short time Hall met another lawyer John McLean, who measured up to the dress, charm, and intellect of Hall's Pittsburgh and Philadelphia friends. By the time Hall had met other townspeople he found McLean to be considered a man of importance and a power in state politics.

Naturally as pioneers pushed farther into the West, hardships made them tough. Otherwise they would have failed to survive their battles with man and nature. Shippers swore amazingly as they cursed their luck when pork spoiled in the flatboats after a long haul. And ruffians defied the law in enormous numbers. In fear of attack, travelers carried concealed weapons for protection. Yet Hall plunged into his new life with enthusiasm and hope.

Only sixteen days after his arrival at Shawneetown, he was editing the town's newspaper. He quickly seized the chance to buy a half-interest in the *Illinois Gazette,* then owned by Henry Eddy. Within five months after his arrival Hall had formed a law partnership with John McLean. When the Illinois General Assembly convened for the first time at Vandalia on December 4, 1820, Hall suspended printing operations for at least eight weeks. One can reasonably assume that he went with John McLean, speaker of the Illinois House of Representatives, to see the new statehouse at Vandalia and to meet the state legislators. Perhaps at this time he met Governor Shadrach Bond. At any rate, Hall's competence was bruited abroad, for Bond named him circuit attorney of the Fourth Judicial Circuit in February, 1821. Certainly as a law-enforcement officer, Hall made his mark. In prosecuting desperadoes, he risked personal danger, but nothing deterred him from seeing justice done. As prosecuting attorney he won the first murder trial in the state. In December, 1824, the Illinois Legislature appointed Hall judge of the Fourth Circuit. He remained in that position until 1827 when the legislators abolished the five judgeships. Thereafter he was known as Judge Hall during the rest of his life.

When he entered the social life of Shawneetown, he took considerable pleasure in the company of the Posey family. In February, 1823, he married Mary Harrison Posey of Walnut Spring, a large plantation near Henderson, Kentucky. During their residence in Shawneetown three children were born to them. Conscientious in her household duties, Mary was satisfied with only the best she could do for her husband and three little ones. She knew well the life of an affluent plantation family. Yet she assumed her role as mistress of their simple house as if she were living at her father's estate, proud of her ancestors and acres. A woman of attractive appearance, she had the gentle manners of a well-bred Kentucky lady.

When General Lafayette visited Illinois in 1825 and stopped at Shawneetown, Judge Hall was chosen to give the address of welcome. The townspeople had recognized the judge's eloquent powers and sharp intellect. People within the state had also acknowledged his ability. Two years later he was elected state treasurer. In the spring of 1827, he moved his family to the wilderness capital. In Vandalia, Judge Hall played an important role in literary activities. As a professional writer he had a regular outlet for his work. The *Port Folio, Illinois Gazette,* and *Illinois Intelligencer* had serialized the notes recorded on his Ohio River journey and his observations of the new state of Illinois. Finally, in 1828 *Letters from the West* came out in book form, published by the London firm of Henry Colburn. Hall actually signed the volume as a "young gentleman," withholding his own name. The publishers, however, changed it to the "Honorable Judge Hall"—a grievous mistake, according to the author. Some who reviewed the volume pounced heavily upon it. They maintained that he had written in a florid style, lied about the climate, and observed scenes and inhabitants without the talent to describe them appropriately. One critic objected to "a venerable judge" kissing the girls and dancing with them so merrily. Hall writhed under the scoff and determined to have no reprints of the book. It was not published in the United States until 1967.

In 1828 he also compiled the *Western Souvenir,* the first annual to contain writings of Western authors. He followed the vogue of publishing a giftbook at Christmas time. Although he begged for contributors and published work by Morgan Neville and Timothy Flint, he actually had to write two-fifths of the material himself. He dressed it up in a bright silk cover, embellished the book with engravings, and included short stories and verses.

Frontiersmen were adept at entertaining themselves, especially by telling stories at the fireside. Some of their tales were woven around the desire to get rich quick. Others told of perseverance and ingenuity in time of danger. Still others suggested the individuality, independence, and self-sufficiency of the early American. Hall believed that these stories should be allowed to take their place within the pages of a book. His annual provided the vehicle. Hall contributed nineteen poems and five prose tales. Included are some of his better known poems—"The New Souvenir," which introduces the giftbook, "To Mary," "The Forest Chief," "The Shawanoe Warrior," and "The Indian Maid's Death Song."

Some of his best known stories, namely, "The French Village," "The Indian Hater," and "Pete Featherton" appeared in the annual. When Mary Russell Mitford prepared an English anthology of American stories, she included those three and another by Hall entitled "The Captain's Lady." No other author was represented by so many tales in *Stories of American Life; by American Writers*. Miss Mitford omitted the work of Washington Irving since it was characterized as European. Other anthologists like Rufus Griswold and the Duyckinck brothers later chose Hall's work as representative of the best American writing.

The publication of *Letters from the West* and the *Western Souvenir* established Hall among frontier writers. While he performed his duties as state treasurer, he continued to spend considerable time writing prose fiction and verses. Then in 1829 he bought a half-interest in the *Illinois Intelligencer,* which promised another outlet for his writing. During the next three years he edited the newspaper, the first in Illinois (it had changed names a number of times since 1814). It still retained its prestige because of regularity of appearance, quality of reporting, and competent management. Under Hall's guidance it even took on a special literary quality. One critic remarked that the editor managed village news "with a genial coffee-house urbanity."

As an active leader in the cultural movements of early Illinois, Judge Hall filled prominent civic positions. In a surprising number of ways he contributed to Western culture—as a lawyer, circuit judge, prosecuting attorney, state treasurer, town trustee, president of the first state historical society, vice-president of the state lyceum, speaker at educational meetings and lyceums, founder and trustee of an early college, and vice-president of the Illinois Colonization Society. As an officer in the last-named organization, he made a strong anti-slavery statement. Some historians have mistakenly discredited the judge as holding pro-slavery views.

One example of Hall's leadership appears appropriate at this point. In an effort to chronicle the history of the state, a group of twenty-five prominent men of the state met on December 8, 1827, in Vandalia to organize a historical society. The group adopted Hall's resolution that it be called "The Antiquarian and Historical Society of Illinois." At the second meeting Judge Hall was elected president.

In his address he urged the members to go to the original sources of information. He attached importance to the life of the people. The history of the government appeared in the records, but many pioneer deeds and achievements would otherwise be forgotten unless recorded by the society. Furthermore, the Potawatomi and Kickapoo tribes were then passing through the settled parts of Illinois. By observing them, the members of the society had the advantage of contributing firsthand to the history and present condition of the Indian tribes. "The French settlements in this state present another attractive subject," the judge suggested. Robert Blackwell, editor and publisher of the *Intelligencer* at that time, referred to the "excellent address of its President, Judge Hall." In fact, he included the complete speech on the first page of the issue of December 22, 1827.

Unfortunately the state historical society which these men founded ceased to function at Hall's departure from Vandalia. A second one was organized at a meeting in the Hall of Representatives of the present Vandalia Statehouse on Saturday, February 4, 1837. A committee of prominent men was appointed to procure materials and aid John Mason Peck in the preparation of the history of Illinois. Unfortunately this society dissolved. Not until sixty-two years later was a third state historical society formed. In 1974 the Illinois State Historical Society celebrated its seventy-fifth anniversary at Vandalia.

Like Poe, the ambition to have his own magazine obsessed Hall, and eventually he obtained enough funds to launch one. *The Illinois Monthly Magazine* deserved its title inasmuch as it provided information about the new state. It ran for twenty-four numbers until September, 1832. Since Vandalia was so remote from other literary activity and shortages of ink and paper were frequent, Hall is to be admired for undertaking the publication.

In its pages he displayed a reformer's zeal for fair treatment of the American Indian. He hoped to see him have security and a place to live. In fact, the protest against the white man's treatment of the Indian characterizes much of his writing. Every chance that offered he befriended the red man both in editorials and short stories. During the Indian uprising of 1832 in Illinois, the judge refused to take up arms against Black Hawk, whom he very much respected.

Constantly Hall advocated public education for all. He insisted that colleges be established for the training of teachers who ought to be given adequate salaries. Without education for all, he argued, the success of a free government is jeopardized. In 1829 he served as a trustee of Illinois College in Jacksonville. The next year he was instrumental in opening the Vandalia High School. As early as 1831 he helped establish the lyceum, an adult educational movement. Although he was considered the foremost advocate of public education in Illinois, legislators, too, were recognizing the need. With persuasive speech William L. D. Ewing, later the fifth governor of Illinois, was attempting to induce legislators to put into law public education for all. By printing extracts of Ewing's "eloquent address" in the number for May, 1831, Hall hoped that the idea, beginning to smoulder in people's minds, would eventually leap into flame.

Obviously the magazine promoted the literature of the region. In almost every issue Hall urged men to utilize Western characters, themes, and landscapes. Accordingly, using the material at hand, he himself wrote short stories for the periodical such as "Michel de Coucy," "A Silver Mine," "A Legend of Carondelet," "The Useful Man," and "The Intestate." He dealt with recognizable types on the frontier with a surprisingly historical reality. The tone is basically humorous with an undercurrent of irony directed at the boatman, land colonizer, quack doctor, idler, and plantation owner. During the two years (1830–1832) of the *Illinois Monthly Magazine,* the first literary periodical west of Cincinnati, twelve of his short stories appeared in it.

In 1832 Hall collected many of his tales in *Legends of the West,* probably his most successful work. This book of short stories about the frontier settlements captured the flavor and color of the robust and colorful inhabitants in their frontier environment. Nearly half of these tales had been previously printed in his other publications. The book, widely accepted, went into an eighth printing.

In Vandalia, Hall's domestic life brought him happiness. He appreciated the assurance and security of having a loving wife and children. But Hall had his sorrows, too. By the spring of 1830, members of his family in the East had one by one died—his father in 1826, his brother Thomas in 1828, John in 1829, and his mother in 1830. Only his brothers Harrison and Alexander and his sister Hannah were still living. When Harrison planned to publish *Selections from the Writings of Mrs. Sarah Hall,* James wrote the preface for his mother's memorial volume. But the greatest sorrow came when Mary gave birth to their child James. She suffered a fever and eight days later succumbed on the morning of August 18, 1832. The infant son's death followed his mother's within two months. Both lie buried in the State Burial Ground, overlooking the original town of Vandalia. Her grave is marked by a simple ledger inscribed by her husband.

After Mary's death, Hall began making plans to move to Cincinnati. His friends had asked him to take over the editorship of the *Western Monthly Magazine,* which was intended to be a continuation of his Vandalia publication. A few weeks before his departure a public meeting in the statehouse was held. Prominent men of the state paid tribute to his excellent service to Illinois and to his literary talents which had merited for him national recognition.

In Cincinnati, Hall continued to write. In 1833 he published *The Soldier's Bride and Other Tales* and the *Western Reader: A Series of Useful Lessons.* Two years later he collected seven stories in *Tales of the Border.* In 1836 he published *Statistics of the West,* in which he wrote of steamboating and the economic history of the early West. Three volumes of the *History of the Indian Tribes of North America* in collaboration with Thomas L. McKenney were issued in 1836, 1838, and 1844. With three new tales added to those previously printed, Wiley and Putnam, a prominent New York firm, published his last volume of short stories, *The Wilderness and the War Path* in 1846. Finally, *Romance of Western History,* his last book, was published in 1857.

Hall also found interest in community affairs, especially the improvement of waterways and promotion of railroads. In politics he accepted the chairmanship of a committee to promote the candidacy of Zachary Taylor. The judge also belonged to an organization that encouraged American artists. Prominent in educational enterprises, he frequently accepted invitations to speak to college societies. On September 3, 1839, Hall remarried. His second wife was a young widow—Mary Louise Anderson Alexander, whose father, Richard Clough Anderson, had served as a general in the Revolutionary War.

For the first three years of his Cincinnati residence he served as editor of the *Western Monthly Magazine.* In 1836 he accepted a position as cashier of the Commercial Bank and in 1853 became its president.

During these years his income enabled him to live in comfort and ease. His end came on July 5, 1868, at his country home, located twenty miles northeast of Cincinnati.

By profession James Hall was a lawyer. Yet his life illustrates that his self-fulfillment lay in the direction of writing. In fact, he might have remained quite unknown to the world were it not for his ability to write. Obviously he has his faults as a writer. He found difficulty in pruning and condensing. At times he indulged in an extravagance of rhetoric. Hall's work is further marred by sentimentality. When not phrased in the vernacular, his dialogue often suffers from a certain stiffness. Yet one would hardly expect him to invest his characters and scenes with the reality of John Steinbeck. Nor would one expect the lean style of Ernest Hemingway or the trim plots so memorably mastered by Graham Greene. Like Washington Irving, Hall wrote in a leisurely manner but without the economical style of modern short story writers. Reliably he depicted customs and employed descriptive details. And like Irving, he looked at life with irony and amusement, seeing the inconsistencies of men's actions.

Had he spent more time in revision, Hall's stories would have less stylistic flaws. Even his brother John Elihu, who had been a rhetoric professor at the University of Maryland, warned him to employ more simplicity and directness of language. So often he wrote hurriedly with little revision in order to get his magazine into print. And of course literary scholars have pointed out these faults. But one wonders if the critical reaction against him has perhaps gone too far.

At first he moved in the direction of realistic fiction but later avoided describing life's crudities on the frontier. Some readers were revolted by the atrocities of the Harpe brothers depicted in *Letters from the West*. They were shocked at such barbarians spreading death and terror. To be sure, he sensed they would be disturbed. Hence he warns, "These horrid events will sound like fiction to your ears. . . . But it is to be recollected that they happened twenty-seven years ago, in frontier settlements, far distant from the civilized parts of our country." Perhaps the reaction of his readers accounts for the toning down of violence, murder, and barbarities in his later work.

During his residence in Vandalia he wrote some of his best short stories, which give a broad exposure to such types of frontiersmen as the quack doctor, religious circuit rider, Indian hater, voyageur, emigrant, boastful hunter, Indian warrior, and descendants of the colonial French. The story of "Pete Featherton" reveals amusing folklore elements. On one particular trip through the forest the boastful hunter encounters a stranger who warns him against trailing the deer. The stranger breathes upon Pete's gun and charms it. But Pete follows an Indian doctor's specific instructions and breaks the spell. In "The Legend of Carondelet," the quack doctor, although spurned by the villagers for courting more than one girl at a time, answers their call. He accidentally brings quick relief to a woman with a fishbone in her throat. Similarly the French ferryman at St. Charles on the Missouri River and the postmaster who carries his office in his hat move realistically in "The Silver Mine."

An especially attractive character in "The French Village" is the voyageur and soldier Baptiste Menou, who has made several hunting expeditions with friendly Indians and has acted as guide and interpreter to the commandant on numerous voyages. The villagers maintain a cordial relationship with their Indian neighbors, with whom they carry on a trade in furs. In exchange they give the Indians trinkets and goods obtained at St. Louis. At the age of forty, the tall, handsome Menou resolves to wed Jeannette Duval. The celebration of charivari, which follows the marriage, the characters, and setting are all drawn from life.

In "The Useful Man," Jemmy Gossamer, who abandons the thought of being educated because useful knowledge would be superfluous, was a very real frontier character. If one would be useful, Jemmy argued, he must deal with yardsticks and have dirty fingers. Henceforth he abandons school, dresses well, plays billiards, and attends the theatre. Still he is not accepted as a gentleman. Troubled by his lack of progress, he realizes he must do something. In conclusion, he becomes a useful man.

Hall sketched vividly Prairie du Rocher, Carondelet, and Fort de Chartres as he depicted the French settlements on the Mississippi River. Photographically he pictured prairies, trees, and flowers. Experiences which Hall drafted into his stories like Bangs's silver witching, Dr. Jeremy Geode's use of the Kickapoo panacea, or Timothy Tompkinson's device of the magic rim for cures were all very close to life on the frontier. Moreover, frontiersmen hated paper money, a subject which occasionally appears in his stories. Unsuccessfully farmers demanded gold and silver coins for their tangible produce. Some inhabitants even went into debt because they had no hard money to meet demands of creditors. In using such themes, Hall demonstrated that the West possessed the materials for realistic fiction.

Indeed Hall deserves a permanent place in the chronology of American literature. It was largely through his efforts that literary activity moved westward across the Appalachians and out to the Mississippi Valley. Of course Louis Hennepin, Pierre Gabriel Marest, Morris Birkbeck, John Mason Peck, and others had written accounts of travel and settlements which contained vivid details. And Timothy Flint, a Harvard graduate who set out for the West in 1815, produced realistic pictures of the frontier in his novels and biographies. But since Hall wrote short stories, verse, essays, biographical sketches, valuable accounts of early life, and a novel, one can credit him as the first important literary figure west of Cincinnati. Moreover, since he published the first Western annual, the first literary periodical in Illinois, and a collection of notable short stories of the region, he is probably the most versatile of all the writers. Beyond question, Hall's short stories deserve more recognition than they have generally received in American literature.

BIBLIOGRAPHY

Burtschi, Mary. "A Memorial to James Hall," *Outdoor Illinois,* V (July, 1966), 18–23.
——. *A Port Folio for James Hall.* Vandalia: Vandalia Historical Society, 1968.
——. "Shawneetown Journey," *Outdoor Illinois,* VIII (October, 1969), 8–15.
——. *Vandalia: Wilderness Capital of Lincoln's Land.* Vandalia: The Little Brick House, 1972.
Flanagan, John T. "Folklore in the Stories of James Hall," *Midwest Folklore,* V (Fall, 1955), 159–168.
——. *James Hall, Literary Pioneer of the Ohio Valley.* Minneapolis: University of Minnesota Press, 1941.
——. "James Hall, Pioneer Editor and Publicist," *Journal of the Illinois State Historical Society,* XLVIII (Summer, 1955), 119–136.
Johannsen, Robert W. "History of the Illinois Frontier: Early Efforts to Preserve the State's Past," *Journal of the Illinois State Historical Society,* LXVIII (April, 1975), 121–142.
Randall, Randolph C. *James Hall, Spokesman of the New West.* Columbus: Ohio State University Press, 1964.
Shultz, Esther. "James Hall in Vandalia," *Journal of the Illinois State Historical Society,* XXIII (April, 1930), 92–112.

THE FRENCH VILLAGE.

On the borders of the Mississippi may be seen the remains of an old French village, which once boasted a numerous population of as happy and as thoughtless souls as ever danced to a violin. If content is wealth, as philosophers would fain persuade us, they were opulent; but they would have been reckoned miserably poor by those who estimate worldly riches by the more popular standard. Their houses were scattered in disorder, like the tents of a wandering tribe, along the margin of a deep bayou, and not far from its confluence with the river, between which and the town was a strip of rich alluvion, covered with a gigantic growth of forest trees. Beyond the bayou was a swamp, which, during the summer heats, was nearly dry, but in the rainy season presented a vast lake of several miles in extent. The whole of this morass was thickly set with cypress, whose interwoven branches, and close foliage, excluded the sun, and rendered this as gloomy a spot as the most melancholy poet ever dreamt of. And yet it was not tenantless—and there were seasons when its dark recesses were enlivened by notes peculiar to itself. Here the young Indian, not yet entrusted to wield the tomahawk, might be seen paddling his light canoe among the tall weeds, darting his arrows at the paroquets that chattered among the boughs, and screaming and laughing with delight as he stripped their gaudy plumage. Here myriads of mosquitoes filled the air with an incessant hum, and thousands of frogs attuned their voices in harmonious concert, as if endeavouring to rival the sprightly fiddles of their neighbours; and the owl, peeping out from the hollow of a blasted tree, screeched forth his wailing note, as if moved by the terrific energy of grief. From this gloomy spot, clouds of miasm rolled over the village, spreading volumes of bile and dyspepsia abroad upon the land; and sometimes countless multitudes of mosquitoes, issuing from the humid desert, assailed the devoted village with inconceivable fury, threatening to draw from its inhabitants every drop of French blood which yet circulated in their veins. But these evils by no means dismayed, or even interrupted the gaiety of this happy people. When the mosquitoes came, the monsieurs lighted their pipes, and kept up not only a brisk fire, but a dense smoke, against the assailants; and when the fever threatened, the priest, who was also the doctor, flourished his lancet, the fiddler flourished his bow, and the happy villagers flourished their heels, and sang, and laughed, and fairly cheated death, disease, and the doctor, of patient and of prey.

Beyond the town, on the other side, was an extensive prairie—a vast unbroken plain of rich green, embellished with innumerable flowers of every tint, and whose beautiful surface presented no other variety than here and there a huge mound—the venerable monument of departed ages—or a solitary tree of stinted growth, shattered by the blast, and pining alone in the gay desert. The prospect was bounded by a range of tall bluffs, which overlooked the prairie—covered at some points with groves of timber, and at others exhibiting their naked sides, or high, bald peaks, to the eye of the beholder. Herds of deer might be seen here at sunrise, slyly retiring to their coverts, after rioting away the night on the rich pasturage. Here the lowing kine lived, if not in clover, at least in something equally nutritious; and here might be seen immense droves of French ponies, roaming untamed, the common stock of the village, ready to be reduced to servitude by any lady or gentleman who chose to take the trouble.

With their Indian neighbours the inhabitants had maintained a cordial intercourse, which had never yet been interrupted by a single act of aggression on either side. It is worthy of remark, that the French have invariably been more successful in securing the confidence and affection of the Indian tribes than any other nation. Others have had leagues with them, which, for a time, have been faithfully observed; but the French alone have won them to the familiar intercourse of social life, lived with them in the mutual interchange of kindness; and, by treating them as friends and equals, gained their entire confidence. This result, which has been attributed to the sagacious policy of their government, is perhaps more owing to the conciliatory manners of that amiable people, and the absence among them of that insatiable avarice, that boundless ambition, that reckless prodigality of human life, that unprincipled disregard of public and solemn leagues, which, in the conquests of the British and the Spaniards, have marked their footsteps with misery, and blood, and desolation.

This little colony was composed, partly, of emigrants from France, and partly of natives—not Indians—but *bona fide* French, born in America; but preserving their language, their manners, and their agility in dancing, although several generations had passed away since their first settlement. Here they lived perfectly happy, and well they might—

for they enjoyed, to the full extent, those three blessings on which our declaration of independence has laid so much stress—life, liberty, and the pursuit of happiness. Their lives, it is true, were sometimes threatened by the miasm aforesaid; but this was soon ascertained to be an imaginary danger. For whether it was owing to their temperance, or their cheerfulness, or their activity, or to their being acclimated, or to the want of attraction between French people and fever, or to all these together—certain it is, that they were blessed with a degree of health only enjoyed by the most favoured nations. As to liberty, the wild Indian scarcely possessed more; for, although the "grand monarque" had not more loyal subjects in his wide domains, he had never condescended to honour them with a single act of oppression, unless the occasional visits of the commandant could be so called; who sometimes, when levying supplies, called upon the village for its portion, which they always contributed with many protestations of gratitude for the honour conferred on them. And as for happiness, they pursued nothing else. Inverting the usual order, to enjoy life was their daily business, to provide for its wants an occasional labour, sweetened by its brief continuance and its abundant fruit. They had a large body of land around the village, held in parcels by individuals, to whom it was granted by the crown. Most of this was allowed to remain in open pasturage; but a considerable tract, including the lands of a number of individuals, was inclosed in a single fence, and called the "common field," in which all worked harmoniously, though each cultivated his own acres. They were not an agricultural people, further than the rearing of a few esculents for the table made them such; relying chiefly on their large herds, and on the produce of the chase, for support. With the Indians they drove an amicable, though not extensive, trade for furs and peltry; giving them in exchange merchandise and trinkets, which they procured from their countrymen at St. Louis. To the latter place they annually carried their skins, bringing back a fresh supply of goods for barter, together with such articles as their own wants required; not forgetting a large portion of finery for the ladies, a plentiful supply of rosin and catgut for the fiddler, and liberal presents for his reverence, the priest.

If this village had no other recommendation, it is endeared to my recollection as the birth-place and residence of Monsieur Baptiste Menou, who was one of its principal inhabitants when I first visited it. He was a bachelor of forty, a tall, lank, hard-featured personage, as straight as a ramrod, and almost as thin, with stiff, black hair, sunken cheeks, and a complexion a tinge darker than that of the aborigines. His person was remarkably erect, his countenance grave, his gait deliberate; and when to all this be added an enormous pair of sable whiskers, it will be admitted that Mons. Baptiste was no insignificant person. He had many estimable qualities of mind and person, which endeared him to his friends, whose respect was increased by the fact of his having been a soldier and a traveller. In his youth he had followed the French commandant in two campaigns; and not a comrade in the ranks was better dressed, or cleaner shaved, on parade than Baptiste, who fought, besides, with the characteristic bravery of the nation to which he owed his lineage. He acknowledged, however, that war was not as pleasant a business as is generally supposed. Accustomed to a life totally free from constraint, the discipline of the camp ill accorded with his desultory habits. He complained of being obliged to eat, and drink, and sleep, at the call of the drum. Burnishing a gun, and brushing a coat, and polishing shoes, were duties beneath a gentleman; and, after all, Baptiste saw but little honour in tracking the wily Indians through endless swamps. Besides, he began to have some scruples as to the propriety of cutting the throats of the respectable gentry whom he had been in the habit of considering as the original and lawful possessors of the soil. He therefore proposed to resign, and was surprised when his commander informed him that he was enlisted for a term, which was not yet expired. He bowed, shrugged his shoulders, and submitted to his fate. He had too much honour to desert, and was too loyal, and too polite, to murmur; but he, forthwith, made a solemn vow to his patron saint, never again to get into a scrape from which he could not retreat whenever it suited his convenience. It was thought that he owed his celibacy, in some measure, to this vow. He had since accompanied the friendly Indians on several hunting expeditions, towards the sources of the Mississippi, and had made a trading voyage to New Orleans. Thus accomplished, he had been more than once called upon by the commandant to act as a guide, or an interpreter—honours which failed not to elicit suitable marks of respect from his fellow villagers, but which had not inflated the honest heart of Baptiste with any unbecoming pride; on the contrary, there was not a more modest man in the village.

In his habits, he was the most regular of men. He might be seen at any hour of the day, either sauntering through the village, or seated in front of his own door, smoking a large pipe formed of a piece of buck-horn, curiously hollowed out, and lined with tin; to which was affixed a short stem of cane from the neighbouring swamp. This pipe was his inseparable companion; and he evinced towards it a constancy which would have immortalized his name, had it been displayed in a better cause. When he walked abroad, it was to stroll leisurely from door to door, chatting familiarly with his neighbours, patting the white-haired children on the head, and continuing his lounge until he had peregrinated the village. His gravity was not a "mysterious carriage of the body to conceal the defects of the mind," but a constitutional seriousness of aspect, which covered as happy and as humane a spirit as ever existed. It was simply a want of sympathy between his muscles and his brains; the former utterly refusing to express any agreeable sensation which might haply titillate the organs of the latter. Honest Baptiste loved a joke, and uttered many and good ones; but his rigid features refused to smile even at his own wit—a circumstance which I am the more particular in mentioning, as it is not common. He had an orphan niece, whom he had reared from childhood to maturity,—a lovely girl, of whose beautiful complexion a poet might say, that its roses were cushioned upon ermine. A sweeter flower bloomed not upon the prairie, than Gabrielle Menou. But as she was never afflicted with weak nerves, dyspepsia, or consumption, and had but one avowed lover, whom she treated with uniform kindness, and married with the consent of all parties, she has no claim to be considered as the heroine of this history. That station will be cheerfully awarded, by every sensible reader, to the more important personage who will be presently introduced.

Across the street, immediately opposite to Mons. Baptiste, lived Mademoiselle Jeanette Duval, a lady who resembled him in some respects, but in many others was his very antipode. Like him, she was cheerful, and happy, and single—but unlike him, she was brisk, and fat, and plump. Monsieur was the very pink of gravity; and Mademoiselle was blessed with a goodly portion thereof,—but hers was specific gravity. Her hair was dark, but her heart was light; and her eyes, though black, were as brilliant a pair of orbs as ever beamed upon the dreary solitude of a bachelor's heart. Jeanette's heels were as light as her heart, and her tongue as active as her heels; so that, notwithstanding her rotundity, she was as brisk a Frenchwoman as ever frisked through the mazes of a cotillion. To sum her perfections, her complexion was of a darker olive than the genial sun of France confers on her brunettes, and her skin was as smooth and shining as polished mahogany. Her whole household consisted of herself and a female negro servant. A spacious garden, which surrounded her house, a pony, and a herd of cattle, constituted, in addition to her personal charms, all the wealth of this amiable spinster. But with these she was rich, as they supplied her table without adding much to her cares. Her quadrupeds, according to the example set by their superiors, pursued their own happiness, without let or molestation, wherever they could find it—waxing fat or lean, as nature was more or less bountiful in supplying their wants; and when they strayed too far, or when her agricultural labours became too arduous for the feminine strength of herself and her sable assistant, every monsieur of the village was proud of an occasion to serve Mam'selle. And well they might be; for she was the most notable lady in the village, the life of every party, the soul of every frolic. She participated in every festive meeting, and every sad solemnity. Not a neighbour could get up a dance, or get down a dose of bark, without her assistance. If the ball grew dull, Mam'selle bounced on the floor, and infused new spirit into the weary dancers. If the conversation flagged, Jeanette, who occupied a kind of neutral ground between the young and the old, the married and the single, chatted with all, and loosened all tongues. If the girls wished to stroll in the woods, or romp on the prairie, Mam'selle was taken along to keep off the wolves and the rude young men; and, in respect to the latter, she faithfully performed her office by attracting them around her own person. Then she was the best neighbour and the kindest soul! She made the richest soup, the clearest coffee, and the neatest pastry in the village; and, in virtue of her confectionary, was the prime favourite of all the children. Her hospitality was not confined to her own domicil, but found its way, in the shape of sundry savoury viands, to every table in the vicinity. In the sick chamber she was the most assiduous nurse, her step was the lightest, and her voice the most cheerful—so that the priest must inevitably have become jealous of her skill, had it not been for divers plates of rich soup, and bottles of cordial, with which she conciliated his favour, and purchased absolution for these and other offences.

Baptiste and Jeanette were the best of neighbours. He always rose at the dawn, and, after lighting his pipe, sallied forth into the open air, where Jeanette usually made her appearance at the same time; for there was an emulation of long standing between them, which should be the earliest riser.

"Bon jour! Mam'selle Jeanette," was his daily salutation.

"Ah! bon jour! bon jour! Mons. Menou," was her daily reply.

Then, as he gradually approximated the little paling which surrounded her door, he hoped Mam'selle was well this morning; and she reiterated the kind enquiry, but with increased emphasis. Then Monsieur enquired after Mam'selle's pony, and Mam'selle's cow, and her garden, and every thing appertaining to her, real, personal, and mixed; and she displayed a corresponding interest in all concerns of her kind neighbour. These discussions were mutually beneficial. If Mam'selle's cattle ailed, or if her pony was guilty of any impropriety, who so able to advise her as Mons. Baptiste? and if his plants drooped, or his poultry died, who so skilful in such matters as Mam'selle Jeanette? Sometimes Baptiste forgot his pipe, in the superior interest of the "tête à tête," and must needs step in to light it at Jeanette's fire, which caused the gossips of the village to say, that he purposely let his pipe go out, in order that he might himself go in. But he denied this; and, indeed, before offering to enter the dwelling of Mam'selle on such occasions, he usually solicited permission to light his pipe at Jeanette's sparkling eyes—a compliment at which, although it had been repeated some scores of times, Mam'selle never failed to laugh and curtsey with great good humour and good breeding.

It cannot be supposed that a bachelor of so much discernment could long remain insensible to the galaxy of charms which centred in the person of Mam'selle Jeanette; and, accordingly, it was currently reported that a courtship, of some ten years standing, had been slyly conducted on his part, and as cunningly eluded on hers. It was not averred that Baptiste had actually gone the fearful length of offering his hand, or that Jeanette had been so imprudent as to discourage, far less reject, a lover of such respectable pretensions. But there was thought to exist a strong hankering on the part of the gentleman, which the lady had managed so skilfully as to keep his mind in a kind of equilibrium, like that of the patient animal between the two bundles of hay—so that he would sometimes halt in the street, midway between the two cottages, and cast furtive glances, first at the one, and then at the other, as if weighing the balance of comfort; while the increased volumes of smoke, which issued from his mouth, seemed to argue that the fire of his love had other fuel than tobacco, and was literally consuming the inward man. The wary spinster was always on the alert on such occasions, manœuvring like a skilful general according to circumstances.

If honest Baptiste, after such a consultation, turned on his heel, and retired to his former cautious position at his own door, Mam'selle rallied all her attractions, and by a sudden demonstration drew him again into the field; but if he marched with an embarrassed air towards her gate, she retired into her castle, or kept shy, and, by able evolutions, avoided everything which might bring matters to an issue. Thus the courtship continued longer than the siege of Troy, and Jeanette maintained her freedom, while Baptiste, with a magnanimity superior to that of Agamemnon, kept his temper, and smoked his pipe in good humour with Jeanette and all the world.

Such was the situation of affairs when I first visited this village, about the time of the cession of Louisiana to the United States. The news of that event had just reached this sequestered spot, and was but indifferently relished. Independently of the national attachment which all men feel, and the French so justly, the inhabitants of this region had reason to prefer, to all others, the government which had afforded them protection without constraining their freedom, or subjecting them to any burthens; and with the kindest feelings towards the Americans, they would willingly have dispensed with any nearer connection than that which already existed. They, however, said little on the subject; and that little was expressive of their cheerful acquiescence in the honour done them by the American people, in buying the country, which the emperor had done them the honour to sell.

It was on the first day of the Carnival that I arrived in the village, about sunset, seeking shelter only for the night, and intending to proceed on my journey in the morning. The notes of the violin, and the groups of gaily attired people who thronged the street, attracted my attention, and induced me to enquire the occasion of this merriment. My host informed me that a "king ball" was to be given at the house of a neighbour, adding the agreeable intimation, that strangers were always expected to attend without invitation. Young and ardent, little persuasion was required to induce me to change my dress, and hasten to the scene of festivity. The moment I entered the room, I felt that I was welcome. Not a single look of surprise, not a glance of more than ordinary attention, denoted me as a stranger or an unexpected guest. The gentlemen nearest the door bowed as they opened a passage for me through the crowd, in which for a time I mingled, apparently unnoticed. At length a young gentleman, adorned with a large nosegay, approached me, invited me to join the dancers, and, after enquiring my name, introduced me to several females, among whom I had no difficulty in selecting a graceful partner. I was passionately fond of dancing, so that, readily imbibing the joyous spirit of those around me, I advanced rapidly in their estimation. The native ease and elegance of the females, reared in the wilderness and unhacknied in the forms of society, surprised and delighted me as much as the amiable frankness of all classes. By and by the dancing ceased, and four young ladies of exquisite beauty, who had appeared during the evening to assume more consequence than the others, stood alone on the floor. For a moment their arch glances wandered over the company who stood silently around, when one of them, advancing to a young gentleman, led him into the circle, and, taking a large bouquet from her own bosom, pinned it upon the left breast of his coat, and pronounced him "KING!" The gentleman kissed his fair elector, and led her to a seat. Two others were selected almost at the same moment. The fourth lady hesitated for an instant, then advancing to the spot where I stood, presented me her hand, led me forward, and placed the symbol on my breast, before I could recover from the surprise into which the incident had thrown me. I regained my presence of mind, however, in time to salute my lovely consort; and never did king enjoy, with more delight, the first fruits of his elevation—for the beautiful Gabrielle, with whom I had just danced, and who had so unexpectedly raised me, as it were, to the purple, was the freshest and fairest flower in this gay assemblage.

This ceremony was soon explained to me. On the first day of the Carnival, four self-appointed kings, having selected their queens, give a ball, at their own proper costs, to the whole village. In the course of that evening the queens select, in the manner described, the kings for the ensuing day, who choose their queens, in turn, by presenting the nosegay and the kiss. This is repeated every evening in the week;—the kings, for the time being, giving the ball at their own expense, and all the inhabitants attending without invitation. On the morning after each ball, the kings of the preceding evening make small presents to their late queens, and their temporary alliance is dissolved. Thus commenced my acquaintance with Gabrielle Menou, who, if she cost me a few sleepless nights, amply repaid me in the many happy hours for which I was indebted to her friendship.

I remained several weeks at this hospitable village. Few evenings passed without a dance, at which all were assembled, young and old;

the mothers vying in agility with their daughters, and the old men setting examples of gallantry to the young. I accompanied their young men to the Indian towns, and was hospitably entertained. I followed them to the chase, and witnessed the fall of many a noble buck. In their light canoes I glided over the turbid waters of the Mississippi, or through the labyrinths of the morass, in pursuit of water fowl. I visited the mounds, where the bones of thousands of warriors were mouldering, overgrown with prairie violets and thousands of nameless flowers. I saw the moccasin snake basking in the sun, the elk feeding on the prairie; and returned to mingle in the amusements of a circle, where, if there was not Parisian elegance, there was more than Parisian cordiality.

Several years passed away before I again visited this country. The jurisdiction of the American government was now extended over this immense region, and its beneficial effects were beginning to be widely disseminated. The roads were crowded with the teams, and herds, and families of emigrants, hastening to the land of promise. Steamboats navigated every stream, the axe was heard in every forest, and the plough broke the sod whose verdure had covered the prairie for ages.

It was sunset when I reached the margin of the prairie on which the village is situated. My horse, wearied with a long day's travel, sprung forward with new vigour when his hoof struck the smooth, firm road which led across the plain. It was a narrow path, winding among the tall grass, now tinged with the mellow hues of autumn. I gazed with delight over the beautiful surface. The mounds and the solitary trees were there, just as I had left them, and they were familiar to my eye as the objects of yesterday. It was eight miles across the prairie, and I had not passed half the distance when night set in. I strained my eyes to catch a glimpse of the village, but two large mounds, and a clump of trees which intervened, defeated my purpose. I thought of Gabrielle, and Jeanette, and Baptiste, and the priest—the fiddles, dances, and French ponies; and fancied every minute an hour, and every foot a mile, which separated me from scenes and persons so deeply impressed on my imagination.

At length I passed the mounds, and beheld the lights twinkling in the village, now about two miles off, like a brilliant constellation in the horizon. The lights seemed very numerous—I thought they moved, and at last discovered that they were rapidly passing about. "What can be going on in the village?" thought I—then a strain of music met my ear—"they are going to dance," said I, striking my spurs into my jaded nag, "and I shall see all my friends together." But as I drew near a volume of sounds burst upon me, such as defied all conjecture. Fiddles, flutes and tambourines, drums, cow-horns, tin trumpets, and kettles, mingled their discordant notes with a strange accompaniment of laughter, shouts, and singing. This singular concert proceeded from a mob of men and boys who paraded through the streets, preceded by one who blew an immense tin horn, and ever and anon shouted, "Cha-ri-va-ry! Charivary!" to which the mob responded, "Charivary!" I now recollected to have heard of a custom which prevails among the American French, of serenading, at the marriage of a widow or widower, with such a concert as I now witnessed; and I rode towards the crowd, who had halted before a well-known door, to ascertain who were the happy parties.

"Charivary!" shouted the leader.

"Pour qui?" said another voice.

"Pour Mons. Baptiste Menou, il est marié!"

"Avec qui?"

"Avec Mam'selle Jeanette Duval—Charivary!"

"Charivary!" shouted the whole company, and a torrent of music poured from the full band—tin kettles, cow-horns and all.

The door of the little cabin, whose hospitable threshold I had so often crossed, now opened, and Baptiste made his appearance—the identical, lank, sallow, erect personage, with whom I had parted several years before, with the same pipe in his mouth. His visage was as long and as melancholy as ever, except that there was a slight tinge of triumph in its expression, and a bashful casting down of the eye—reminding one of a conqueror, proud but modest in his glory. He gazed with an embarrassed air at the serenaders, bowed repeatedly, as if conscious that he was the hero of the night, and then exclaimed—

"For what you make this charivary?"

"Charivary!" shouted the mob; and the tin trumpets gave an exquisite flourish.

"Gentlemen!" expostulated the bridegroom, "for why you make this charivary for me? I have never been marry before—and Mam'selle Jeanette has never been marry before!"

Roll went the drum!—cow-horns, kettles, tin trumpets, and fiddles, poured forth volumes of sound, and the mob shouted in unison.

"Gentlemen! pardonnez-moi—" supplicated the distressed Baptiste.

"If I understan dis custom, which have long prevail vid us, it is vat I say—ven a gentilman, who has been marry before, shall marry de second time—or ven a lady have de misfortune to loose her husban, and be so happy to marry some odder gentilman, den we make de charivary—but 'tis not so wid Mam'selle Duval and me. Upon my honour we have never been marry before dis time!"

"Why, Baptiste," said one, "you certainly have been married, and have a daughter grown."

"Oh, excuse me, sir! Madame St. Marie is my niece; I have never been so happy to be marry, until Mam'selle Duval have do me dis honneur."

"Well, well! it's all one. If you have not been married, you ought to have been, long ago:—and might have been, if you had said the word."

"Ah, gentilmen, you mistake."

"No, no! there's no mistake about it. Mam'selle Jeanette would have had you ten years ago, if you had asked her."

"You flatter too much," said Baptiste, shrugging his shoulders;—and finding there was no means of avoiding the charivary, he, with great good humour, accepted the serenade, and, according to custom, invited the whole party into his house.

I retired to my former quarters, at the house of an old settler—a little, shrivelled, facetious Frenchman, whom I found in his red flannel night-cap, smoking his pipe, and seated like Jupiter in the midst of clouds of his own creating.

"Merry doings in the village!" said I, after we had shaken hands.

"Eh, bien! Mons. Baptiste is marry to Mam'selle Jeanette."

"I see the boys are making merry on the occasion."

"Ah, sacré! de dem boy! they have play hell to night."

"Indeed! how so?"

"For make dis charivary—dat is how so, my friend. Dis come for have d' Americain government to rule de countrie. Parbleu! they make charivary for de old maid and de old bachelor!"

I now found that some of the new settlers, who had witnessed this ludicrous ceremony without exactly understanding its application, had been foremost in promoting the present irregular exhibition, in conjunction with a few degenerate French, whose love of fun outstripped their veneration for their ancient usages. The old inhabitants, although they joined in the laugh, were nevertheless not a little scandalised at the innovation. Indeed, they had good reason to be alarmed; for their ancient customs, like their mud-walled cottages, were crumbling to ruins around them, and every day destroyed some vestige of former years.

Upon enquiry, I found that many causes of discontent had combined to embitter the lot of my simple-hearted friends. Their ancient allies, the Indians, had sold their hunting grounds, and their removal deprived the village of its only branch of commerce. Surveyors were busily employed in measuring off the whole country, with the avowed intention, on the part of the government, of converting into private property those beautiful regions which had heretofore been free to all who trod the soil or breathed the air. Portions of it were already thus occupied. Farms and villages were spreading over the country with alarming rapidity, deforming the face of nature, and scaring the elk and the buffalo from their long frequented ranges. Yankees and Kentuckians were pouring in, bringing with them the selfish distinctions and destructive spirit of society. Settlements were planted in the immediate vicinity of the village; and the ancient heritage of the ponies was invaded by the ignoble beasts of the interlopers. Certain pregnant indications of civil degeneration were alive in the land. A county had been established, with a judge, a clerk, and a sheriff; a court-house and jail were about to be built; two lawyers had already made a lodgment at the county site; and a number of justices of the peace, and constables, were dispersed throughout a small neighbourhood of not more than fifty miles in extent. A brace of physicians had floated in with the stream of population, and several other persons of the same cloth were seen passing about, brandishing their lancets in the most hostile manner. The French argued very reasonably from all these premises—that a people who brought their own doctors expected to be sick, and that those who commenced operations in a new country, by providing so many engines and officers of justice, must certainly intend to be very wicked and litigious. But when the new comers went the fearful length of enrolling them in the militia; when the sheriff, arrayed in all the terrors of his office, rode into the village, and summoned them to attend the court as jurors; when they heard the judge enumerate to the grand jury the long list of offences which fell within their cognizance;—these good folks shook their heads, and declared that this was no longer a country for them.

From that time the village began to depopulate. Some of its inhabitants followed the footsteps of the Indians, and continue, to this day, to trade between them and the whites—forming a kind of link between civilised and savage men. A larger portion, headed by the priest, floated down the Mississippi, to seek congenial society among the sugar plantations of their countrymen in the south. They found a pleasant spot on the margin of a large bayou, whose placid stream was enlivened by droves of alligators, sporting their innocent gambols on its surface. Swamps, extending in every direction, protected them from further intrusion. Here a new village arose, and a young generation of French was born, as happy and as careless as that which is passing away.

Baptiste alone adhered to the soil of his fathers, and Jeanette, in obedience to her marriage vow, cleaved to Baptiste. He sometimes talked of following his clan, but when the hour came he could never summon fortitude to pull up his stakes. He has passed so many happy years of single blessedness in his own cabin, and had been so long accustomed to view that of Jeanette with a wistful eye, that they had become necessary to his happiness. Like other idle bachelors, he had had his daydreams, pointing to future enjoyment. He had been, for years, planning the junction of his domains with those of his fair neighbour; had arranged how the fences were to intersect, the fields to be enlarged, and the whole to be managed by the thrifty economy of his partner. All these plans were now about to be realised; and he wisely concluded that he could smoke his pipe, and talk to Jeanette, as comfortably here as elsewhere; and as he had not danced for many years, and Jeanette was growing rather too corpulent for that exercise, he reasoned that even the deprivation of the fiddles and king balls could be borne. Jeanette loved comfort too; but having, besides, a sharp eye for the main chance, was governed by a deeper policy. By a prudent appropriation of her own savings, and those of her husband, she purchased from the emigrants many of the fairest acres in the village, and thus secured an ample property.

A large log house has since been erected in the space between the cottages of Baptiste and Jeanette, which form wings to the main building, and are carefully preserved in remembrance of old times. All the neighbouring houses have fallen down, and a few heaps of rubbish, surrounded by corn fields, show where they stood. All is changed, except the two proprietors, who live here in ease and plenty, exhibiting, in their old age, the same amiable character, which, in early life, won for them the respect and love of their neighbours and of each other.

THE INDIAN HATER.

Some years ago, I had occasion to travel over the beautiful prairies of Illinois, then a frontier state, containing but few inhabitants, and those chiefly of the class called backwoodsmen. In the course of my journey, I stopped one day at a village to rest; and while my horse was eating his corn, and mine hostess was picking the chicken that was to be broiled for my dinner, I stepped into a neighbouring store to purchase some small article of which I stood in need. I found a number of persons there, engaged, some in buying merchandise, some in talking politics, and others in reading the manuscript advertisements of stray horses and constable's sales, that were pasted on the walls. There were a bottle of whiskey and a pitcher of water on the counter, free for all comers, as was the hospitable fashion of those days, before temperance had got to be a tip-top virtue, or Father Mathew the greatest of modern reformers. Being not unwilling to observe a scene which might afford amusement, and to while away a few minutes in conversation, I leaned my back against the counter, and addressed myself to a person having the appearance of a substantial farmer, who answered my inquiries respecting the country with intelligence and civility.

While thus engaged, my attention was drawn to a person who stood near. He was a man who might have been about fifty years of age. His height did not exceed the ordinary stature, and his person was rather slender than otherwise; but there was something in his air and features which distinguished him from common men. The expression of his countenance was keen and daring. His forehead was elevated, his cheek bones high, his lips thin and compressed. Long exposure to the climate had tanned his complexion to a deep brown, and had hardened his skin and muscles, so as to give him the appearance of a living petrifaction. He seemed to have lived in the open air, exposed to the elements, and to every extreme of temperature.

There was nothing in the dress of this individual to attract attention; he was accosted occasionally by others, and seemed familiar with all who were present. Yet there was an air of abstraction, and standing aloof about him, so different from the noisy mirth and thoughtless deportment of those around him, that I could not help observing him. In his eye there was something peculiar, yet I could not tell in what that peculiarity consisted. It was a small grey orb, whose calm, bold, direct glances, seemed to vouch that it had not cowered with shame, or quailed in danger. There was blended in that eye a searching keenness, with a quiet vigilance—a watchfull, sagacious self-possession—so often observable in the physiognomy of those who are in the habit of expecting, meeting, and overcoming peril. His heavy eyebrows had been black, but time had touched them with his pencil. He was dressed in a coarse grey hunting shirt, of homespun cotton, girded round the waist with a broad leathern belt, tightly drawn, in which rested the long knife, with which the western hunter despatches his game, cuts his food, picks his flint and his teeth, and whittles sticks for amusement.

Upon the whole, there was about this man an expression of quiet determination, of grim and gloomy sternness, of intense but smothered passion, which stamped him as something out of the ordinary view of character; yet there were indications of openness and honesty, that forbade distrust. He was rough, but not a ruffian. His was not the unblushing front of hardy guilt, nor the lurking glance of underhanded villany. A stranger would not have hesitated to confide in his faith or courage, but would have been extremely reluctant to provoke his hostility.

I had barely time to make these observations, when several Indians, who had strolled into the village, entered the store. The effect of their presence upon the backwoodsman, whom I have described, was instantaneous and remarkable. His eyes rolled wildly, as if he had been suddenly stung to madness, gleaming with a strange fierceness—an intense lustre, like that which flashes from the eyeballs of the panther, when crouched in a dark covert, ready to dart upon his prey. His sallow cheek was flushed; the muscles, that but a moment before seemed so rigid, became flexible, and twitched convulsively. His hand sliding quietly to the hilt of his large knife, as if by an involuntary impulse, grasped it firmly; and it was easy to perceive that a smothered fire had been disturbed, and that a single breath would be sufficient to light up a blaze. But, except these indications, he remained motionless as a statue, gazing with a look of intense ferocity at the intruders. The Indians halted when their eyes met his, and exchanged glances of intelligence with each other. Whether it was from instinct, or that they knew the man, or whether the natural sagacity of their race enabled them to read the signs of danger in his scowling visage, they seemed willing to avoid him, and retired. The backwoodsman made a motion, as if to follow;

but several of the company, who had watched this silent, though momentary scene, with interest, gently withheld him, and after conversing with him a few moments in an earnest, but under tone, led him off in one direction, while the Indians rode away in another.

Having understood from the farmer, with whom I had been talking, that he was about to return home, and that my route led through his neighbourhood, I accepted the offer of his company and guidance, and we set out together. It was a pleasant afternoon in the fall, and as our horses trotted quietly over the smooth prairie road, the discourse naturally fell upon the scene we had just witnessed, and I expressed a curiosity to learn something of the history and character of the man, whose image had impressed itself so forcibly on my mind. I was young and romantic then, and singular as this being certainly was, his peculiarities were probably magnified to my excited fancy.

"He is a strange, mysterious-looking being," said I, "and I should think he must be better, or worse than other men."

"Samuel Monson is a very good neighbour," replied the farmer, cautiously.

"You say that in a tone," rejoined I, "which seems to imply, that in some other respects he may not be so good."

"Well—as to that, I cannot say, of my own knowledge, that I know any harm of the man."

"And what do other people say of him?"

The farmer hesitated, and then, with a caution very common among people of this description, replied:

"People often say more than they can prove. It's not good, no how, to be talking of one's neighbours; and Monson, as I said before, is a good neighbour."

"But a bad man, as I understand."

"No—far from it—the man's well enough—"

My companion hesitated here, as gossips of both sexes are apt to do, when conscious of a strong inclination to tell all they know on a delicate subject; but my laudable thirst for useful knowledge had, I suppose, awakened a benevolent desire to gratify it, and the worthy man added, in a low tone, and looking cautiously around:

"—Except—The folks do say he are rather too keen with his rifle."

"How so? does he shoot his neighbour's cattle?"

"No, sir—Samuel Monson is as much above a mean action as any other man."

"What then, is he quarrelsome?"

"Oh, bless you, no! There's not a peaceabler man in the settlement; but he used to be a great Indian fighter in the last war, and he got sort o' haunted to the woods; and folks do say that he's still rather too keen on the track of a moccasin."

"I do not exactly understand you, my dear sir.—The Indians are now quiet, I believe, and at peace with us?"

"Why yes, they are very peaceable. They never come near us, except now and then a little party comes in to trade. There's not many of them in these parts, and they live a good piece off."

"They are civil and harmless, are they not?"

"Yes, sir, quite agreeable—bating the killing of a hog once in a while—but that we don't vally—it is but just nateral to the poor savage to shoot anything that runs in the woods. They have a honing in that way, and you can't stop them, no way you can fix it."

"In what way, then, does this Monson interfere with them?"

"I did not say, stranger, that Monson done it. No, no; I would'n't hurt no man's character; but the fact and the truth are about this: now and then an Indian are missing; and now and then one are found dead in the range;—and folks will have their notions, and their talk, and their suspicions about it—and some talk hard of Monson."

"But why charge it upon him?"

"Well, if you must have it out, stranger,—in this country we all know the bore of every man's rifle. Monson's gun carries just fifty to the pound. Now the bullet holes in all these Indians that have been shot are the same, and we know whose rifle they suit. Besides this, horse tracks have been seen on the trail of the moccasin. They were very particular tracks, and just suited the hoof of a certain horse. Then a certain man was known to be lying out in the range, about that same time; and when all these things are put together, it don't take a Philadelphia lawyer to tell who done the deed. No mistake in Sam Monson. He likes a skrimmage with them. He goes off sometimes, and is gone for weeks, and people reckon that he goes to their own hunting grounds to lie in wait for them. They do say, he can scent a red-skin like a hound, and never lets a chance slip—no how."

"But is it possible, that in a civilized country, within the reach of our laws, a wretch is permitted to hunt down his fellow-creatures like wild beasts; to murder a defenceless Indian, who comes into our territory in good faith, believing us to be what we profess, as a Christian people!"

"Well, stranger,—as to the matter of that—it is not exactly permitted; we don't know for certain who does it, and it's not any particular man's business to inquire into it, more than another. There's no love for the Indians among us, no how. Many of the people have had their kin murdered by the savages in early times; and all who have been raised in the back woods, have been learned to dislike them, and fear them. The Monson is an honest fellow, works hard, pays his debts, and is always willing to do a good turn, and it would seem hard to break neighbourhood with him for the matter of a few Indians. People don't think the Indians of much account, no how!"

"But the wickedness of such unprovoked murder—the shame—the breach of law, the violation of hospitality!"

"Well, so it is. It are a sin; and sorry would I be to have it on my conscience. But, then, some think an Indian or so will never be missed; others, again, hate to create an interruption in the settlement; others, who pretend to know the law, say that the general government has the care of the business of the Indians, and that our state laws won't kiver the case—so they allow it's none of our business. Some folks, you know, go in heavy for state rights, and don't believe in meddling with any thing that belongs to Uncle Sam; and withal Monson keeps his own counsel, and so among hands he goes his own road, and no questions asked."

All this seemed very strange to me. Border wars, we all know, are productive of feuds, which are implacable and lasting. Predatory incursions, which hardly attract the notice of the government, bring carnage and devastation, ruin and sorrow, to the fireside. Private property is wasted, and the war is against individuals, rather than the public. The actors in each scene are identified; men and families feel the sense of personal injury, and hatred and revenge are the consequence. But I was not aware that such a state of feeling existed on our own frontier. While these thoughts passed through my mind, we rode forward in silence, which was broken by my inquiring what injury this individual had suffered from the Indians, which could justify him in thus destroying them with impunity.

"Injury enough!" replied my companion: "to tell the plain sentimental truth, he has cause enough to hate them; and many a man that would not dip his own hand in the blood of an Indian, would as soon die as betray him; for few of us could lay our hands upon our hearts and say we would not do the same in his situation."

At this point of the conversation we were joined by several horsemen, who were pursuing the same road with ourselves, and joined us, in accordance with the gregarious habits of the country, which induce men to prefer a larger company to a smaller, on all occasions; and my companion being unwilling to pursue the subject in their hearing, I was unable to learn from him what injury the Indian hater had received, to provoke his sanguinary career of vengeance. Nor did another opportunity occur; for we soon came to a point where the roads diverging, obliged us to separate, and although my friendly fellow-traveller, with the usual hospitality of the country, invited me to take up my lodgings at his house for the night, I was obliged to decline the invitation, and we parted.

I continued my journey into the northwestern part of Illinois, which was then just beginning to attract the attention of settlers, and contained but few inhabitants. Delighted with this beautiful wilderness, unspoiled by art, and retaining all its native loveliness, and wishing to explore the lands lying between this tract and the Wabash, I determined, on my return, to strike directly across, through a district of country in which there were as yet no settlements, of about one hundred and fifty miles in extent. I hired an Indian guide, who was highly recommended to me, and set out under his protection.

It is not easy to describe the sensations of a traveller, unaccustomed to such scenery, on first beholding the vast prairies, which I was about to explore. Those I had heretofore seen were comparatively small; both are unique, and highly attractive, but as they differ in their features and scenic effect, I shall endeavour to describe them separately.

The smaller prairies, or those in which the plain and woodland alternate frequently, are the most beautiful. The points of woodland which make into them like so many capes or promontories, and the groves which are interspersed like islands, are in these lesser prairies always sufficiently near to be clearly defined to the eye, and to give the scene an interesting variety. We see plains, varying from a few hundred acres to several miles in extent, not perfectly level, but gently rolling or undulating, like the swelling of the ocean when nearly calm. The graceful curve of the surface is seldom broken, except when, here and there, the eye rests upon one of those huge mounds, which are so pleasing to the poet, and so perplexing to the antiquarian. The whole is overspread with grass and flowers, constituting a rich and varied carpet, in which a ground of lively green is ornamented with a profusion of the gaudiest hues, and fringed with a rich border of forest and thicket. Deep recesses in the edge of the timber resemble the bays and inlets of a lake; while occasionally a long vista, opening far back into the forest, invites the eye to roam off and refresh itself, with the calm beauty of a distant perspective.

The traveller, as he rides along over these smaller prairies, finds his eye continually attracted to the edges of the forest, and his imagination employed in tracing the beautiful outline, and in finding out resemblances between these wild scenes and the most tastefully embellished productions of art. The fairest pleasure-grounds, the noblest parks of European noblemen and princes, where millions have been expended to captivate the senses with Elysian scenes, are but mimic representations, on a reduced scale, of the beauties which are here spread by nature; for here are clumps and lawns, groves and avenues, the tangled thicket, and the solitary tree, the lengthened vista, and the secluded nook, and all the varieties of scenic attraction, but on a plan so extensive, as to offer a wide scope, and an endless succession of changes, to the eye.

There is an air of refinement here, that wins the heart,—even here, where no human residence is seen, where no foot of man intrudes, and where not an axe has ever trespassed on the beautiful domain. It is a wilderness shorn of every savage association, a desert that "blossoms as the rose." So different is the feeling awakened from anything inspired by mountain or woodland scenery, that the instant the traveller emerges from the forest into the prairie, he feels no longer solitary. The consciousness that he is travelling alone, and in a wilderness, escapes him; and he indulges in the same pleasing sensations which are enjoyed by one who, having lost his way, and wandered bewildered among the labyrinths of a savage mountain, suddenly descends into rich and highly cultivated plains, and sees around him the delightful indications of taste and comfort. The gay landscape charms him. He is encompassed by the refreshing sweetness and graceful beauty of the rural scene; and recognises at every step some well-remembered spot, or some ideal paradise in which the fancy had loved to wander, enlarged and beautified, and, as it were, retouched by nature's hand. The clusters of trees so fancifully arranged, the forest outline so gracefully curved, seem to have been disposed by the hand of taste, for the enjoyment of intelligent beings; and so complete is the illusion, that it is difficult to dispel the belief that each avenue leads to a village, and each grove conceals a splendid mansion.

Widely different was the prospect exhibited by the more northern and central districts of the State. Vast in extent, the distant forest was either beyond the reach of the eye, or was barely discernible in the shapeless outline of blue, faintly impressed on the horizon. As the smaller prairies resembled a series of larger and lesser lakes, so these boundless plains remind one of the ocean waste. Here and there a solitary tree, torn by the wind, stood alone like a dismantled mast in the ocean. As I followed my guide through this lonely region, my sensations were similar to those of the voyager, when his bark is launched upon the sea. Alone, in a wide waste, with my faithful pilot only, I was dependent on him for support, guidance, and protection. With little to diversify the path, and nothing to please the eye but the carpet of verdure, which began to pall upon the sense, a feeling of dreariness crept over me—a desolation of the spirit, such as one feels when crossed in love, or when very drowsy on a hot afternoon, after a full dinner. But these are feelings which, like the sea-sickness of the young mariner, are soon dispelled. I began to find a pleasure in gazing over this immense, unbroken waste, in watching the horizon under the vague hope of meeting a traveller, and in following the deer with my eyes as they galloped off—their agile forms growing smaller and smaller as they receded, until they shrunk into nothing. Sometimes I descried a dark spot at an immense distance, and pointed it out to my companion with a joy like that of the seaman who discovers a sail in the distant speck which floats on the ocean. When such an object happened to be in the direction of our path, I watched it with interest as it rose and enlarged upon the vision—supposing it at one moment to be a solitary horseman, and wondering what manner of man he would turn out to be—at another supposing it might be a wild animal, or a wagon, or a pedestrian; until, after it had seemed to approach for hours, I found it to be a tree.

Nor was I entirely destitute of company; for my Pottowottomie guide proved to be both intelligent and good-humoured; and although his stock of English was but slender, and his habit of taciturnity somewhat confirmed, his conversational powers, when exerted, were quite respectable. His knowledge of the country was extensive and accurate, so that he was able, not only to choose the best route, but to point out all the localities. When we halted he kindled a fire, spread my pallet, and formed a shelter to protect me from the weather. When we came to a stream which was too deep to ford, he framed a raft to cross me over, with my baggage, while he mounted my horse and plunged into the water. Throughout the journey, his assiduities were as kind and unremitting as all his arrangements were sagacious and considerate. A higher motive than the mere pecuniary reward which he expected for his services governed his actions. He considered himself my companion; not only responsible for my safety, as a matter of contract, but kindly interested for my comfort. A genuine integrity of purpose, a native politeness and manliness of deportment, raised him above the ordinary savage, and rendered him not only a respectable, but an interesting man.

After travelling nearly five days without beholding a human habitation, we arrived at the verge of a settlement on the Wabash. We passed along a rich bottom, covered with huge trees, whose limbs were hung with immense grape vines, and whose thick shade afforded a strong contrast to the scenes we had left behind us, and then ascending a gentle rise, stood on a high bluff bank of the Wabash. A more secluded and beautiful spot has seldom been seen. A small river, with a clear stream, rippling over a rocky bed, meandered round the point on which we stood, and then turning abruptly to the left, was lost among the trees. The opposite shore was low, thickly wooded, and beautifully rich in the variety of mellow hues painted by the autumn sun.

The spot we occupied was a slip of table land, a little higher than the surrounding country. It had once been cleared for cultivation, but was now overgrown with hazel bushes, vines, and briars, while a few tall, leafless trunks, once the proudest oaks of the forest, weather-beaten and blackened by fire, still adhered tenaciously to the soil. A heap of rubbish, intermingled with logs half burnt and nearly rotten, showed the remains of what had once been a chimney, and indicated the spot where a cabin had stood, the residence of human beings—but all else had been destroyed by time or fire. We gazed on the ruins of a desolated homestead, but many years seemed to have rolled away since it had been inhabited. The clearing had been of small extent; it was now covered with a rank vegetation, which was fast restoring it to the dominion of the wilderness. One spot only, which had probably been the yard in front of the little dwelling, and had been beaten hard, was covered with a smooth green sward, unmixed with weeds or brush; and here we stood gazing at this desolate spot, and that beautiful river. It was but a moment, and neither of us had broken silence, when the crack of a rifle was heard, and my guide, uttering a dismal yell, fell at my feet.

Recovering his senses for an instant, he grasped his gun, partly raised his body, and cast upon me a look of reproach, which I shall never forget; and then, as if satisfied by the concern and alarm of my countenance, and my prompt movement to assist him, he gave me one hand, and pointing with the other towards the woods, exclaimed—"Bad—bad, white man!—take care"—and expired. The aim had been unerring—the bullet had penetrated deep in a vital spot, and life was extinguished in a moment.

I was so much surprised and shocked at this fatal catastrophe, that I stood immoveable, thoughtless of my own safety, mourning over the stout Indian, my kind and worthy guide, who lay weltering in his gore, when I was startled by a slight rustling in the bushes close behind me, and as I turned with an involuntary shudder, a backwoodsman, rifle in hand, issued from the covert. Advancing hastily, without the least appearance of shame or fear, until he came to the corpse, and paying not the slightest attention to me, he stood and gazed sternly at the fallen warrior. It was Monson! The fierce and gloomy picture, which had been impressed so indelibly upon my memory, stood before me in living presentation, his hand imbrued in blood, and his soul freshly steeped in murder.

"There's another of the cursed crew gone to his last account!" he exclaimed. "He is not the first, and he shall not be the last.—It's an old debt, but it shall be paid to the last drop!"

As he spoke, he gnashed his teeth, and his eyes gleamed with the malignity of gratified revenge. Then turning to me, and observing the deep abhorrence with which I shrunk back, he said gruffly,

"May be, stranger, you don't like this sort of business."

"Wretch—miscreant—murderer! begone! Approach me not," I exclaimed, shrinking back in disgust and terror, and drawing a large pistol from my belt; but, before I was aware, the backwoodsman, with a sudden spring, caught my arm, and wrested the weapon from me; and then remaining perfectly calm, while I was ready to burst with rage, he proceeded:

"This is a poor shooting-iron for a man to have about him—it might do for young men to tote in a settlement, but it's of no use in the woods—no more than a shot-gun."

"Scoundrel!" said I, "you shall repent your violence—"

"Young man!" interrupted he, very coolly, "I am no scoundrel, no more than yourself; you mistake, you do not know me."

"Murderer!" repeated I, "for such I know you to be. My life is in your power, but I dread not your vengeance! If I live, this bloody deed shall not go unpunished!"

While I was thus exhausting myself, in the expression of my rage and horror, the more politic Monson, having possessed himself of the Indian's gun, dropped it, together with my unlucky pistol, on the ground, and placing one foot on them, proceeded deliberately to load his rifle.

"Don't be alarmed, young man," said he, in reply to my last remark, "I shall not hurt a hair of your head. You cannot provoke me to it. I never harmed a Christian man, to my knowledge!"

But although his habitual command of his temper enabled him to treat the matter thus coolly, he was evidently under high excitement, and as he finished loading his piece, he exclaimed, "See here!" Then pointing to the ruins of the cabin, he proceeded in a hurried tone.

"This was my home. Here I built a house with my own labour. With the sweat of my brow I opened this clearing. Here I lived with my wife, my children, and my mother. We worked hard—lived well—and were happy."

His voice became choked; he paused, as if overcome by the recollections of the past; but after a moment's hesitation, he proceeded with the simple and vehement eloquence of passion:

"I am a rough man, stranger, but I have feelings like other men. My blood is up now, and I will tell you a tale that will explain this deed. One night—it was in the fall—just at this season—I had gathered my corn, ready for shucking, the labour of the year was done, and I was sitting by the fire with my family, with the prospect of plenty and comfort around me—when I heard the Indian yell! I never was a coward, but I knew that sound too well; and when I looked round upon the women and helpless babes, that depended on me for protection, a cold chill ran over me, and my heart seemed to die. I ran to the door, and beheld my stacks in a blaze. I caught up my gun—but in a moment a gang of yelling savages came pouring in at my door, like so many howling wolves. I fired, and one of them fell—I caught up an axe and rushed at them with such fury that I cleared the cabin. The vile varments then set fire to the roof, and we saw the flames spreading around us. What could I do?

"Stranger, you never were in such a fix, and you don't know how a man feels. Here was my poor old mother, and my wife, and my little children, unable to fight, or to escape. I burst open the door, and rushed madly out; but they pushed me back. The yelling wretches were determined to burn us in our house. The blazing timbers came falling among us—my wife hung on my neck, and called on me to save our children—our pious old mother prayed—the savage butchers roared, and laughed, and mocked us. They caught my dog, that we loved as one of the family, hung him, and then threw his carcass among us.

"I grasped my axe, and rushed out again—hoping to beat them back, until the neighbours could be alarmed, and come to our assistance. I killed several of them; but they overpowered me, bound me, and led me up to witness the ruin of all that was dear to me. Wife—children—mother—all, all perished here in the flames before my eyes. They perished in lingering torments—screaming with terror—racked with pain. I saw their agonies—heard their cries—they called on my name. Tied hand and foot, what could I do? Oh Heaven, can I ever forget it!"

The man of sorrows paused in his tragical narrative, overcome by the tender and terrible recollections that it called forth. He looked wildly around. Tears came to his relief—that hard, ferocious misanthrope, the fountains of whose tenderness seemed to have been long since broken and dried up, melted at the recital of his own griefs. Nature had resumed her sway over him. The pause was but brief; when, brushing the tears from his rough visage, he continued:

"They carried me off a prisoner. I was badly wounded, and so heart-broken, that for three days I was helpless as a child. Then a desire of revenge grew up in my heart, and I got strong. I gnawed the strings they had bound me with, and escaped from them in the night. I thought that God had spared me to be a scourge to the savage. The war with the Indians broke out soon afterwards, and I joined every expedition—I was foremost in every fight; but I could not quench my thirst for the blood of the miscreants. I swore never to forgive them, and when peace came, I continued to make war. I have made it a rule to kill every red-skin that came in my way; my revenge is not yet satisfied, and so long as I have strength to whet my knife on a stone, or ram a ball into my rifle, I shall continue to slay the savage!

"As for this fellow," he continued, "I would not have troubled him, any where else, if I had seen him in your company. I would not harm nor trouble any christian man, especially a stranger. But when he came *here,* setting his cursed feet on *this soil*—stepping over the ruins of my homestead, and the ashes of my family—when he intruded upon me as I sat here alone, thinking over the fate of my poor wife and children, it was not my nater to spare him—I couldn't do it.

"Let us part friends, young man, I have done you no harm; if I have hurt your feelings, I ask your pardon. Pursue your own way, and leave me to mine. If you have a grey-headed mother that prays for you, a wife and children that love you—they will welcome you, and you will be happy. I am alone;—there is none to mourn with me, no one to rejoice at my coming. When all that you cherish is torn from you in one moment, by hellish ruffians, condemn me if you can: but not till then.—That path will lead you to a house."

PETE FEATHERTON.

Every country has its superstitions, and will continue to have them, so long as men are blessed with lively imaginations, and while any portion of mankind remain ignorant of the causes of natural phenomena. That which cannot be reconciled with experience, will always be attributed to supernatural influence; and those who know little, will imagine much more to exist than has ever been witnessed by their own senses. I am not displeased with this state of things, for the journey of life would be dull indeed, if those who travel it were confined for ever to the beaten highway, worn smooth by the sober feet of experience. To turnpikes, for our beasts of burden, I have no objection; but I cannot consent to the erection of railways for the mind, even though the architect be "wisdom, whose ways are pleasant, and whose paths are peace." It is sometimes agreeable to stray off into the wilderness which fancy creates, to recline in fairy bowers, and to listen to the murmurs of imaginary fountains. When the beaten road becomes tiresome, there are many sunny spots where the pilgrim may loiter with advantage—many shady paths, whose labyrinths may be traced with delight. The mountain, and the vale, on whose scenery we gaze enchanted, derive new charms, when their deep caverns and gloomy recesses are peopled with imaginary beings.

But above all, the enlivening influence of fancy is felt, when it illumines our firesides, giving to the wings of time, when they grow heavy, a brighter plumage, and a more sprightly motion. There are seasons, when the spark of life within us seems to burn with less than its wonted vigour; the blood crawls heavily through the veins; the contagious chillness seizes on our companions, and the sluggish hours roll painfully along. Something more than a common impulse is then required to awaken the indolent mind, and give a new tone to the flagging spirits. If necromancy draws her magic circle, we cheerfully enter the ring; if folly shakes her cap and bells, we are amused; a witch becomes an interesting personage, and we are even agreeably surprised by the companionable qualities of a ghost.

We, who live on the frontier, have little acquaintance with imaginary beings. These gentry never emigrate; they seem to have strong local attachments, which not even the charms of a new country can overcome.

A few witches, indeed, were imported into New England by the Puritans; but were so badly used, that the whole race seems to have been disgusted with new settlements. With them, the spirit of adventure expired, and the weird women of the present day wisely cling to the soil of the old countries. That we have but few ghosts will not be deemed a matter of surprise by those who have observed how miserably destitute we are of accommodations for such inhabitants. We have no baronial castles, nor ruined mansions;—no turrets crowned with ivy, nor ancient abbeys crumbling into decay; and it would be a paltry spirit, who would be content to wander in the forest, by silent rivers and solitary swamps.

It is even imputed to us as a reproach by enlightened foreigners, that our land is altogether populated with the living descendants of Adam—creatures with thews and sinews, who eat when they are hungry, laugh when they are tickled, and die when they are done living. The creatures of romance, say they, exist not in our territory. A witch, a ghost, or a brownie, perishes in America, as a serpent is said to die the instant it touches the uncongenial soil of Ireland. This is true, only in part. If we have no ghosts, we are not without miracles. Wonders have happened in these United States. Mysteries have occurred in the valley of the Mississippi. Supernatural events have transpired on the borders of "the beautiful stream"; and in order to rescue my country from undeserved reproach, I shall proceed to narrate an authentic history, which I received from the lips of the party principally concerned.

A clear morning had succeeded a stormy night in December; the snow laid ankle-deep upon the ground, and glittered on the boughs, while the bracing air, and the cheerful sunbeams, invigorated the animal creation, and called forth the tenants of the forest from their warm lairs and hidden lurking-places.

The inmates of a small cabin on the margin of the Ohio were commencing with the sun the business of the day. A stout, raw-boned forester plied his keen axe, and, lugging log after log, erected a pile on the ample hearth, sufficiently large to have rendered the last honours to the stateliest ox. A female was paying her morning visit to the cow-yard, where a numerous herd of cattle claimed her attention. The plentiful breakfast followed; corn-bread, milk, and venison, crowned the oaken board, while a tin coffee-pot of ample dimensions supplied the beverage which is seldom wanting at the morning repast of the substantial American farmer.

The breakfast over, Mr. Featherton reached down a long rifle from the rafters, and commenced certain preparations, fraught with danger to the brute inhabitants of the forest. The lock was carefully examined, the screws tightened, the pan wiped, the flint renewed, and the springs oiled; and the keen eye of the backwoodsman glittered with an ominous lustre, as its glance rested on the destructive engine. His blue-eyed partner, leaning fondly on her husband's shoulder, essayed those coaxing and captivating blandishments, which every young wife so well understands, to detain her husband from the contemplated sport. Every pretext was urged with affectionate pertinacity, which female ingenuity could supply:—the wind whistled bleakly over the hills, the snow lay deep in the valleys, the deer would surely not venture abroad in such bitter cold weather, the adventurous hunter might get his toes frost-bitten, and her own hours would be sadly lonesome in his absence. He smiled in silence at the arguments of his bride, for such she was, and continued his preparations, with the cool, but good-natured determination of one who is not to be turned from his purpose.

He was indeed a person with whom such arguments, except the last, would not be very likely to prevail. Mr. Peter Featherton, or as he was familiarly called by all who knew him, Pete Featherton, was a bold, rattling Kentuckian, of twenty-five, who possessed the characteristic peculiarities of his countrymen—good and evil—in a striking degree. His red hair and sanguine complexion, announced an ardent temperament; his tall form, and bony limbs, indicated an active frame inured to hardships; his piercing eye and high cheek bones, evinced the keenness and resolution of his mind. He was adventurous, frank, and social—boastful, credulous, illiterate, and at times wonderfully addicted to the marvellous. His imagination was a warm and fruitful soil, in which "tall oaks from little acorns grew," and his vocabulary was overstocked with superlatives. He loved his wife—no mistake about that—but next to her his affections entwined themselves about his gun, and expanded over his horse; he was true to his friends, never missed an election day, turned his back upon a frolic, nor affected to dislike a social glass.

He believed that the best qualities of all countries were combined in Kentucky; and had the most whimsical manner of expressing his national attachments. He was firmly convinced that the battle of the Thames was the most sanguinary conflict of the age—"a raal reg'lar skrimmage,"—and extolled Colonel Dick Johnson as a "severe old colt." He would admit freely that Napoleon was a great genius—Metternich,

Castlereagh, "and them fellows" knew "a thing or two," but then they "were no part of a priming to Henry Clay."

When entirely "at himself"—to use his own language—that is to say, when duly sober, Pete was friendly and rational, courteous and considerate, and a better tempered fellow never shouldered a rifle. But he was a social man, who was liable to be "overtaken," and let him get a glass too much, and there was no end to his extravagance. Then it was that his genius bloomed and brought forth strange boasts, and strong oaths, his loyalty to old Kentuck waxed warm, and his faith in his horse, his gun, and his own manhood grew into idolatry. Always bold and self-satisfied, and habitually energetic in the expression of his predelictions, he now became invested with the agreeable properties of the snapping-turtle, the alligator, and the steamboat, and gifted with the most affable and affectionate spirit of auto-biography. It was now that he would dwell upon his own bodily powers and prowess, with the enthusiasm of a devotee, and as the climax of this rhetorical display, would slap his hands together, spring perpendicularly into the air, and after uttering a yell worthy of the stoutest Winnebago, swear that he was "the best man in the country," and "could whip his weight in wild cats," "no two ways about it"—he was "not afraid of no man, no way you could fix it;" and finally, after many other extravagancies, he would urge, with no gentle asseveration, his ability to "ride through a crab-apple orchard on a streak of lightning."

In addition to all this, which one would think was enough for any reasonable man, Pete would sometimes brag that he had the best gun, the prettiest wife, the best-looking sister, and the fastest nag, in all Kentuck; and that no man dare say to the contrary. It is but justice to remark, that there was more truth in this last boast, than is usually found on such occasions, and that Pete had good reason to be proud of his horse, his gun, and his lady love.

These, however, were the happy moments, which are few and far between; they were the brilliant inspirations, playing like the lightning in an overheated atmosphere,—gleaming over the turbid stream of existence, as the meteor flashes through the gloom of the night. When the fit was off, Pete was a quiet, good-natured, listless soul, as one would see on a summer's day—strolling about with a grave aspect, a drawling, and a deliberate gait, a stoop of the shoulders, and a kind of general relaxation of the whole outward and inward man—in a state of entire freedom from restraint, reflection, and want, and without any impulse strong enough to call forth his latent manhood—as the panther, with whom he often compared himself, when his appetite for food is sated, sleeps calmly in his lair, or wanders harmlessly through his native thickets.

Our hero was a farmer, or as the very appropriate phrase is, "made a *crap*" on his own land—for besides making a crop he performed but few of the labours of the husbandman. While planting his corn, tending it, and gathering in the harvest, he worked with a good will; but these, thanks to a prolific soil, and a free country, were all his toils, and they occupied not half of the year, the remainder of which was spent in the more manly and gentlemanly employments of hunting, attending elections, and officiating at horse races. He was a rare hand at a "shucking," a house raising, or a log rolling; merry and strong, he worked like a young giant, and it was worth while to hear the gladsome tones of his clear voice, and the inspiring sound of his loud laugh; while the way he handled the axe, the beauty and keenness of the implement, the weight and precision of the blows, and the gracefulness of the action, were such as are not seen except in the "wilderness," where chopping is an accomplishment as well as the most useful of labours.

It will readily be perceived, that our hunter was not one who could be turned from his purpose by the prospect of danger or fatigue; and a few minutes sufficed to complete his preparations. His feet were cased in moccasins, and his legs in wrappers of dressed deerskin; and he was soon accoutred with a powder horn, quaintly carved all over with curious devices,—an ample pouch with flints, patches, balls, and other "fixens"—and a hunter's knife,—and throwing "Brown Bess," for so he called his rifle, over his shoulder, he sallied forth.

But in passing a store hard by, which supplied the country with gunpowder, whiskey, and other necessaries, as well as with the luxuries of tea, sugar, coffee, calico, calomel, and chandlery, he was hailed by one of the neighbours, who invited him to "light off and take something." Pete said he had "no occasion," but "rather than be nice," he dismounted, and joined a festive circle, among whom the cup was circulating freely. Here he was soon challenged to swap rifles, and being one of those who could not "stand a banter," he bantered back again, without the least intention of parting with his favourite weapon. Making offers, like a skilful diplomatist, which he knew would not be accepted, and feigning great eagerness to accede to any reasonable proposition, while inwardly resolved to reject all, he magnified the perfections of Brown Bess.

"She can do any thing but talk," said he. "If she had legs she could hunt by herself. It is a pleasure to *tote* her—I naterrally believe there is not a rifle south of Green river, that can throw a ball so far, or so true. I can put a bullet in that tree, down the road, a mile off."

"You can't do it, Pete—I'll bet a treat for the whole company."

"No"—said the hunter. "I could do it—but I don't want to strain my gun."

These discussions consumed much time and much whiskey—for the rule on such occasions is, that he who rejects an offer to trade, must treat the company, and thus every point in the negociation costs a pint of spirits.

At length, bidding adieu to his companions, Pete struck into the forest—it was getting late, and he "must look about pretty peart," he said, to get a venison before night. Lightly crushing the snow beneath his active feet, he beat up the coverts, and traversed all the accustomed haunts of the deer. He mounted every hill, and descended into every valley—not a thicket escaped the penetrating glance of his practised eye. Fruitless labour! not a deer was to be seen. Pete marvelled at this unusual circumstance, as the deer were very abundant in this neighbourhood, and no one knew better where to look for them than himself.

But what surprised him still more, was, that the woods were less familiar to him than formerly. He knew them "like a book." He thought he was acquainted with every tree within ten miles of his cabin; but now, although he certainly had not wandered so far, some of the objects around him seemed strange, while others again were faintly recognized; and there was, altogether, a singular confusion in the character of the scenery, which was partly familiar, and partly new; or rather, in which many of the component parts were separately well known, but were so mixed up and changed in relation to each other, as to baffle even the knowledge of an expert woodsman.

The more he looked, the more he was bewildered. Had such a thing been possible, he would have thought himself a lost man. He came to a stream which had heretofore rolled to the west, but now its course pointed to the east; and the shadows of the tall trees, which, according to Pete's experience and philosophy, ought at noon to fall towards the north, all pointed to the south. He looked at his right and his left hands, somewhat puzzled to know which was which; then scratched his head—but scratching the head, though a good thing in its way, will not always get a man out of a scrape. He cast his eye upon his own shadow, which had never deceived him—when lo! a still more extraordinary phenomenon presented itself. It was travelling round him like the shade on a dial—only a great deal faster, as it veered round to all the points of the compass in the course of a single minute. Mr. Peter Featherton was "in a bad fix."

It was very evident too, from the dryness of the snow, and the brittleness of the twigs, which snapped off as he brushed his way through the thickets, that the weather was intensely cold; yet the perspiration was rolling in large drops from his brow. He stopped at a clear spring, and thrusting his hands into the cold water, attempted to carry a portion of it to his lips; but the element recoiled and hissed, as if his hands and lips had been composed of red hot iron. Pete felt quite puzzled when he reflected on all these contradictions in the aspect of nature; and began to consider what act of wickedness he had been guilty of, which could have rendered him so hateful, that the deer fled at his approach, the streams turned back, and the shadows fell the wrong way, or danced round their centre.

He began to grow alarmed, and would have liked to turn back, but was ashamed to betray such weakness, even to himself; and being naturally bold, he resolutely kept on his way. At last, to his great joy he espied the tracks of deer imprinted on the snow; they were fresh signs—and, dashing upon the trail, with the alacrity of a well-trained hound, he pursued, in hopes of soon overtaking the game. Presently he discovered the tracks of a man, who had struck the same trail in advance of him, and supposing it to be one of his neighbours, he quickened his pace, as well to gain a companion, which in the present state of his feelings he so much needed, as to share the spoil with his fellow hunter. Indeed, in his present situation and condition of mind, Pete thought he would be willing to give half of what he was worth, for the sight of a human face.

"I don't like the signs, no how," said he, casting a rapid glance around him; and then throwing his eyes downwards at his own shadow, which had ceased its rotatory motion, and was now swinging backward and forward like a pendulum—"I don't like the signs, no way they can be fixed."

"You are not scared, are you, Pete?" he continued, smiling at the oddity of such a question.

"Oh no, bless your heart, Mr. Featherton, I'm not scared—I'm not of that breed of dogs—there's no back out in me—but then I must say—to speak sentimentally—that I feel sort o' jubus—I do so. But I'll soon see whether other people's shadows act the fool like mine."

Upon further observation, there appeared to be something peculiar in the human tracks before him, which were evidently made by a pair of feet which were not fellows—or were *odd fellows*—for one of them was larger than the other. As there was no person in the settlement who was thus deformed, Pete began to doubt whether it might not be the devil, who in borrowing shoes to conceal his cloven hoofs might have got those that did not match. He stopped, and scratched his head, as many a learned philosopher has done, when placed between the horns of a dilemma less perplexing than that which now vexed the spirit of our hunter. It was said long ago, that there is a tide in the affairs of men; and although our good friend Pete had never seen this sentiment in black and white, yet it is one of those truths, which are written in the heart of every reasonable being, and was only copied by the poet, from the great book of nature, a source from which he was a great borrower. It readily occurred to Pete on this occasion; and as he had enjoyed through life an uninterrupted tide of success, he reflected whether the stream of fortune might not have changed its course, like the brooks he had crossed, whose waters, for some sinister reason, seemed to be crawling up-hill.

He stopped, drew out his handkerchief, and wiped the perspiration from his brow. "This thing of being scared," said he, "makes a man feel mighty queer—the way it brings the sweat out is curious!" And again it occurred to him, that it was incumbent on him to see the end of the adventure, as otherwise he would show a want of that courage, which he had been taught to consider as the chief of the cardinal virtues.

"I can't back out," said he, "I never was raised to it, no how; and if the devil's a mind to hunt in this range, he shan't have all the game."

The falling into the sentimental vein, as one naturally does from the heroic: "Here's this hankercher, that my Polly hemmed for me, and marked the two first letters of my name on it—P. for Pete and F. for Featherton—would she do the like of that for a coward? Could I ever look in her pretty face again, if I was mean enough to be scared? No—I'll go ahead—let what will come."

He soon overtook the person in advance of him, who, as he had suspected, was a perfect stranger. He had halted and was quietly seated on a log, gazing at the sun, when our hunter approached, and saluted him with the usual hearty, "How are you, stranger?" The person addressed made no reply, but continued to gaze at the sun, as if totally unconscious that any other individual was present. He was a small, thin, old man, with a grey beard of about a month's growth, and a long sallow melancholy visage, while a tarnished suit of snuff-coloured clothes, cut after the quaint fashion of some religious sect, hung loosely about his shrivelled person.

Our bold backwoodsman, somewhat awed, now coughed, threw the butt end of his gun heavily upon the frozen ground, and, still failing to elicit any attention, quietly seated himself on the other end of the log occupied by the stranger. Both remained silent for some minutes—Pete with open mouth, and glaring eyeballs, observing his companion with mute astonishment, and the latter looking at the sun.

"It's a warm day, this," said Pete, at length, passing his hand across his brow, as he spoke, and sweeping off the heavy drops of perspiration that hung there. But receiving no answer, he began to get nettled. He thought himself not civilly treated. His native assurance, which had been damped by the mysterious deportment of the person who sat before him, revived. "One man's as good as another"—thought he; and screwing up his courage to the sticking point, he arose, approached the silent man, and slapping him on the back, exclaimed—

"Well, stranger! don't the sun look mighty droll away out there in the north?"

As the heavy hand fell on his shoulder, the stranger slowly turned his face towards Pete, who recoiled several paces,—then rising without paying the abashed hunter any further attention, he began to pursue the trail of the deer. Pete prepared to follow, when the other turning upon him with a stern glance, enquired:

"Who are you tracking?"

"Not you," replied the hunter, whose alarm had subsided when the enemy began to retreat; and whose pride, piqued by the abruptness with which he had been treated, enabled him to assume his usual boldness of manner.

"Why do you follow this trail, then?"

"I trail deer."

"You must not pursue them further, they are mine!"

The sound of the stranger's voice broke the spell, which had hung over Peter's natural impudence, and he now shouted—

"*Your* deer! that's droll too! who ever heard of a man claiming the deer in the woods!"

"Provoke me not,—I tell you they are mine."

"Well, not—you're a comical chap! Why stranger,—the deer are wild! They're jist nateral to the woods here, the same the timber. You might as well say the wolves and the painters are yours, and all the rest of the wild varments."

"The tracks you behold here, are those of wild deer, undoubtedly—but they are mine. I routed them from their bed, and am driving them home."

"Home—where is your home?" inquired Pete, at the same time casting an inquisitive glance at the stranger's feet.

To this home question no reply was given, and Pete, fancying that he had got the best of the altercation, pushed his advantage,—adding sneeringly—

"Could'nt you take a pack or two of wolves along? We can spare you a small gang. It is mighty wolfy about here."

"If you follow any further it is at your peril," said the stranger.

"You don't reckon I'm to be skeered, do you? If you do, you are barking up the wrong tree. There's no back out in none of my breed, no how. You must'nt come over them words agin, stranger."

"I repeat—"

"You had best not repeat—I allow no man to do that to me"—interrupted the irritated woodsman, "You must not imitate the like of that. I'm Virginy born, and Kentucky raised, and drot my skin, if I take the like of that from any man—no, Sir!"

"Desist, rash man, from altercation—I despise your threats!"

"The same to you, Sir!"

"I tell you what, stranger!" continued Pete, endeavouring to imitate the coolness of the other, "as to the vally of a deer or two—I don't vally them to the tantamount of this here cud of tobacco; but I'm not to be backed out of my tracks. So keep off, stranger—don't come fooling about me. I might hurt you. I feel mighty wolfy about the head and shoulders. Keep off, I say, or you might run agin a snag."

With this the hunter "squared himself, and sot his triggers," fully determined either to hunt the disputed game, or be vanquished in combat. To his surprise, the stranger, without appearing to notice his preparations, advanced and blew with his breath upon his rifle.

"Your gun is charmed!" said he. "From this day forward you will kill no deer."

So saying, that mysterious old man, with the most provoking coolness, resumed his way; while Pete remained bewildered; and fancied that he smelt brimstone.

Pete Featherton remained a moment or two lost in confusion. He then thought he would pursue the stranger, and punish him as well for his threats, as for the insult intended to his gun; but a little reflection induced him to change his decision. The confident manner in which that singular being had spoken, together with a kind of vague assurance in his own mind, that the spell had really taken effect, so unmanned and stupefied him, that he quietly "took the back track," and strode homewards. He had not gone far, when he saw a fine buck, half concealed among the hazel bushes which beset his path, and resolved to know at once how matters stood between Brown Bess and the pretended conjurer, he took a deliberate aim, fired,—and away bounded the buck unharmed!

With a heavy heart, our mortified forester re-entered his own dwelling, and replaced his degraded weapon in its accustomed berth under the rafters.

"You have been long gone," said his wife, "but where is the venison you promised me?"

Pete was constrained to confess that he had shot nothing.

"That is strange!" said the lady, "I never knew you fail before."

Pete framed twenty excuses. He had felt unwell—his gun was out of fix—it was a bad day for hunting—the moon was not in the right place—and there were no deer stirring.

Had not Pete been a very young husband, he would have known that the vigilant eye of a wife is not to be deceived by feigned apologies. Female curiosity never sleeps; and the love of a devoted wife is the most sincere and the most absorbing of human passions. Pretty Mrs. Featherton saw, at a glance, that something had happened to her helpmate, more than he was willing to confess; and being quite as tenacious as himself, in her reluctance against being "backed out of her tracks," she determined to bring her inferior moiety to auricular confession, and advanced firmly to her object, until Pete was compelled to own, "That he believed Brown Bess was, somehow—sort o'— charmed."

"Now, Mr. Featherton!" remonstrated his sprightly bride, leaning fondly on his shoulder, and parting the long red locks on his forehead—"are you not ashamed to tell me such a tale as that? Charmed indeed! Ah well, I know how it is. You have been down at the store, shooting for half pints!"

"No, indeed—" replied the husband emphatically, "I wish I may be kissed to death, if I've pulled a trigger for a drop of liquor this day."

Ah, Peter—what a sad evasion was that! Surely the adversary when he blew his breath—sadly sulphureous of smell—upon thy favourite gun, breathed into thee the spirit of lying, of which he is the father. Mrs. Featherton saw farther into a millstone than he was aware of—but she kept her own counsel.

"I believe you, Peter,—you did not *shoot* for it—but do now—that's a dear good soul!—tell me where you have been, and what has happened? You are not well—or something is wrong—for never did Pete Featherton and Brown Bess fail to get a venison any day in the year."

Soothed by this well-timed compliment, and not unwilling to have the aid of counsel in this trying emergency, and to apply to his excited spirit the balm of conjugal sympathy, Pete narrated minutely to his wife all the particulars of his meeting with the mysterious stranger. The lady was all attention; but was as much wonder-struck as Pete himself. She had heard of spells being cast upon guns, and so had Peter—often—but then neither of them had ever known such a case, in their own experience; and although she had recipes for pickling fruit, and preserving life, and preventing various maladies, she knew of no remedy which would remove the spell from a rifle. As she could give no sage advice, she prescribed sage tea, bathing the feet, and going to bed, and Pete submitted passively to all this—not perceiving, however, how it could possibly affect his gun.

When Pete awoke the next morning, the events which we have described appeared to him as a dream; indeed, he had been dreaming of them all night, and it was somewhat difficult to unravel the tangled thread of recollection, so as to separate the realities of the day from the illusions of the pillow. But resolving to know the truth, he seized his gun, and hastened to the woods. Alas! every experiment produced the same vexatious result. The gun was charmed! "No two ways about that!" It was too true to make a joke of; and the hunter stalked harmlessly through the forest.

Day after day he went forth, and returned with no better success. The very deer became sensible of his inoffensiveness, and would raise their heads, and gaze mildly at him as he passed; or throw back their antlers, and bound carelessly across his path. Day after day, and week after week, passed without bringing any change; and Pete began to feel very ridiculously. A harmless man—a fellow with a gun, that could not shoot! he could imagine no situation more miserable than his own. To walk through the woods, to see the game, to come within gun-shot of it, and yet to be unable to kill a deer, seemed to be the height of human wretchedness. He felt as if he was "the meanest kind of a white man." There was a littleness, an insignificance, attached to the idea of not being able to kill a deer, which, to Pete's mind, was downright disgrace. More than once, he was tempted to throw the gun into the river; but the excellence of the weapon, and the recollection of former exploits, restrained him; and he continued to stroll through the woods, firing now and then at a fat buck, under the hope that the charm would expire some time or other, by its own limitation; but the fat bucks continued to treat him with a familiarity amounting to contempt, and to frisk fearlessly in his path.

At length Pete bethought him of a celebrated Indian doctor, who lived at no great distance. We do not care to say much of doctors, as they are a touchy race—and shall therefore touch upon this one briefly. An Indian doctor is not necessarily a descendant of the Aborigines. The title, it is true, originates from the confidence which many of our countrymen repose in the medical skill of the Indian tribes. But to make an Indian doctor a red skin is by no means indispensable. To have been taught by a savage, to have seen one, or, at all events, to have heard of one, is all that is necessary, to enable any individual to practise this lucrative and popular branch of the healing art. Neither is any great proficiency in literature requisite; it is important only to be expert in spell-ing. Your Indian doctor is one who practises without a diploma—the only degree his exhibits, is a high degree of confidence. He neither nauseates the stomach with odious drugs, nor mars the fair proportions of nature with the sanguinary lancet. He believes in the sympathy which is supposed to exist between the body and the mind, which, like the two arms of a syphon, always preserve a corresponding relation to each other; and the difference between him and the regular physician—called in the vernacular of the frontier, the mercury doctor—is that they operate at different points of the same figure—the one practising on the immaterial spirit, while the other grapples with the bones and muscles. I cannot determine which is right; but must award to the Indian doctor at least this advantage, that his art is the most widely beneficial; for while your doctor of medicine restores a lost appetite, his rival can, in addition, recover a strayed or stolen horse. If the former can bring back the faded lustre to a fair maiden's cheeks, the latter remove the spell from a churn or a rifle. The dyspeptic and the dropsical may hie to the disciples of Rush and Wistar, but the crossed-in-love, and lack-a-daysical, find a charm in the practitioner who professes to follow nature.

To a sage of this order, did Pete disclose his misfortune, and apply for relief. The doctor examined the gun, and looked wise; and having measured the calibre of the bore, with a solemnity which was as imposing as it was unquestionably proper on so serious an occasion, directed the applicant to come again.

At the appointed time, the hunter returned, and received from the wise man two balls, one of pink, the other of a silver hue. The doctor instructed him to load his piece with one of these bullets, which he pointed out, and proceed through the woods to a certain secluded hollow, at the head of which was a spring. Here he would see a white fawn, at which he was to shoot. It would be wounded, but would escape, and he was to pursue its trail, until he found a buck, which he was to kill with the other ball. If he accomplished all this accurately, the charm would be broken; but success would depend upon his having faith, keeping up his courage, and firing with precision.

Pete, who was well acquainted with all the localities, carefully pursued the route which had been indicated, treading lightly along, sometimes elated with the prospect of speedily breaking the spell, and restoring his beloved gun to usefulness and respectability—sometimes doubting the skill of the doctor—admiring the occult knowledge of men who could charm and uncharm deadly weapons—and ashamed alternatively of his doubts and his belief. At length he reached the lonely glen; and his heart bounded with delight, as he beheld the white fawn quietly grazing by the fountain. The ground was open, and he was unable to get within his usual distance, before the fawn raised her delicate head, looked timidly around, and snuffed the breeze, as if conscious of the approach of danger. Pete trembled with excitement—his heart palpitated. It was a long shot and a bad chance—but he could not advance a step further, without danger of starting the game—and Brown

Bess could carry a ball farther than that, with fatal effect.

"Luck's a lord," said he, as he drew the gun up to his face, took a deliberate aim, and pulled the trigger. The fawn bounded aloft at the report, and then darted away through the brush, while the hunter hastened to examine the signs. To his great joy he found the blood profusely scattered; and now flushed with the confidence of success, he stoutly rammed down the other ball, and pursued the trail of the wounded fawn. Long did he trace the crimson drops upon the snow, without beholding the promised victim. Hill after hill he climbed, vale after vale he passed—searching every thicket with penetrating eyes; and he was about to renounce the chase, the wizard, and the gun, when lo!—directly in his path, stood a noble buck, with numerous antlers branching over his fine head!

"Aha! my jolly fellow! I've found you at last!" exclaimed the delighted hunter, "you are the very chap I've been looking after. Your blood shall wipe off the disgrace from my charming Bess, that never hung fire, burned priming, nor missed the mark in her born days, till that vile abominable varment blowed his brimstone breath on her! Here goes—"

He shot the buck. The spell was broken—Brown Bess was restored to favour, and Pete Featherton never again wanted venison.

A LEGEND OF CARONDELET.

There is no knowledge so valuable as a knowledge of the world. Thousands have grown gray in the acquisition of learning, without ever getting the slightest insight into the human character, while many seem to be born with an intrinsic perception of the workings of the human heart. There is a something called common sense, which books do not teach, but which, nevertheless, is worth more than all the lore of antiquity. A man may starve with his head full of Latin and Greek, while a single grain of common sense operates like the presence of the prophet of old upon the widow's cruise. The fortunate individual who is born with this desirable quality, bears a charmed existence, and glides along in the voyage of life with an ease that surprises his companions. There is a thriftiness about such persons which is almost miraculous; like those hardy plants that spring up in the crevices of the rock, they flourish in the midst of barrenness, when every thing perishes around them.

To this class belonged Timothy Eleazer Tompkinson, the hopeful heir of a worthy mariner, whose domicil was situated in a small seaport of New England, but who, being almost constantly abroad, was obliged to leave his only son to the care of a maiden aunt and to the teaching of a public school. This amiable youth exhibited, even in childhood, some of the touches of the disposition which adhered to him through life. He liked salt water better than attic wit; and loved to steer his little boat, in the most stormy weather, around the capes and headlands of the neighbouring sea-coast, better than to trace out the labyrinths of a problem, or to wander among the shoals and quicksands of metaphysics. In his tenderest years, he launched his bark upon the ocean with the temerity of a veteran pilot; and when the gay breeze swept along, and the waves danced and sparkled in the sun, his little sail might be seen skimming over the surface like a sea-bird. Often as he strolled off in the morning might the shrill voice of his aunt, the worthy Miss Fidelity Tompkinson, be heard hailing him with, "Where are you going, Timmy dear?" "Don't go near the water, dear;" and as often would he toss his head and march on, smiling at the simplicity of his watchful guardian and marvelling at the timidity of women. In vain did the village pedagogue remind him that time flies swifter than a white squall, and that in the voyage of life there is but one departure, which, if taken wrong, can never be corrected. Tim would listen with a smile, and then placing his tarred hat on one side of his head, stroll off whistling to the beach.

At sixteen it was concluded that the years and gifts of Timothy rendered him a suitable candidate for college honours, and his name was accordingly entered upon the books of a celebrated institution. Here he was soon distinguished; not for Latin or logic, but for cleverness, ingenuity, and gymnastic feats. He never was a great talker, but, on the contrary, expressed himself with a laudable brevity, and with that idiomatic terseness of language which is common along shore, where a significant sea-phrase answers all the purpose of a long argument; and he reasoned, plausibly enough, that one who employed so few words, had little use for any other tongue than his own, which afforded a copious medium for the conveyance of his slender stock of ideas. In the mathematical sciences, he was better skilled. Few could estimate with more accuracy the number of superficial yards between his own chamber and a neighbouring orchard, or calculate with more nicety the difference of distance between these points upon a direct line, or by the meanders of a number of obtuse angles. He knew the exact height of every window in the college edifice, and the precise force required to elevate a projectile from the college green to the roof of the tutor's boarding-house. He knew precisely the angle at which an object could be presented to the retina of a professor's eye, and was acquainted with the depth of every intellect and the measure of every purse in the Senior class. In short, however deficient in Athenian polish, he had all the hardihood of a Spartan youth, and was especially gifted with that thrifty quality called common sense. He was a lucky boy, too. Though foremost in every act of mischief, he was always the last to be found out or punished; and though he never studied, he always managed to glide unnoticed through the college examinations, or to obtain praise for productions which were strongly suspected to be not his own. In difficulty or danger, he was sure to have a device to meet the exigency, and was so often successful on such occasions, that his companions compared him to the active animal, which, when thrown into the air, always lights upon its feet.

It will be readily imagined that our hero gained but few scholastic attainments; yet he was, nevertheless, a general favourite. He was blessed with the finest temper in the world. His good nature was absolutely invincible. Although the very prince of mischief, none suspected him of malice. In the midst of a bitter reproof he would smile in the professor's face; and the student who treated him with insolence was, perhaps, the first to receive some kind act from his hand. If the faculty frowned upon him, he had the *faculty* of turning the storm into sunshine, and of averting punishment by a well-timed jest or compliment. Every body loved Tim, and Tim loved every body. He hated study; but then he liked college, because the students were jolly fellows, and the professors took flattering kindly, and stood quizzing with that patience which is the result of long endurance.

How long these halcyon days would have lasted, and whether the name of Timothy Eleazer Tompkinson would have been numbered among the alumni of the college, is now beyond the reach of conjecture; for just as he had attained his twentieth year, the news came that his father had discharged the debt of nature, leaving all his other debts unpaid, his sister fortuneless, and his son a beggar. Our hero paid the tribute of a tear to the memory of his departed parent, and more than one drop attested his sympathy for the desolate condition of his kind aunt. But he soon brushed the moisture from either eye, and as the good president condoled with him in a tone of sincere affection, he acknowledged with a smile that his case might have been much more desperate.

"The worst of it is," said the reverend principal, "that you will not be able to take out a degree."

"I shall be sorry to quit college," replied the youth, "but as for the degree, that is neither here nor there."

The president shook his head and took snuff, while Tim cast a sidelong glance out of the window, gazing wistfully over the green landscape, which was now decked with the blossoms of spring, and longing to rove uncontrolled about that beautiful world, that seemed so redolent of sunshine, and flowers, and balmy breezes.

"It is a sad thing," said the president, "for a young man to be cast upon the cold charity of the wide world."

"The wider the world is the better," said Tim; "it is a fine thing to have sea-room; and as to its coldness, I don't regard that; a light heart will keep a man warm in the stiffest northeaster that ever blew."

The worthy president applied his handkerchief to his nose, then wiped his spectacles, and wondered how marvellously the wind is tempered to the shorn lamb.

A Legend of Carondelet.

"Thou hast a bold heart," said the president, "still I cannot bear to see you cast forth without a profession."

"Oh, never mind that; I'm all the better without it. To a man without a farthing in his pocket, a profession is only an incumbrance, which forces him to wear good clothes and talk like a book. I shall put out into the world as light as a feather, and float along with the breeze."

Arguments were thrown away upon the common sense of our hero, who was already panting to exercise among men the same devices which had smoothed all the asperities of college life, which had won him the affection of his fellow-students, and gained even the kindness of his superiors.

"There goes," said the president, as he gazed after him, "the shrewdest boy and the greatest dunce that ever left college—the most obstinate, yet the most conciliatory spirit."

Obstinate as he was, there was one point on which he yielded. He abandoned a long-cherished intention of going to sea, upon the earnest solicitation of his aunt. It was the only request from his sole remaining relative. She had nursed his infancy with unceasing kindness; she now leaned upon him for support, and her tears were irresistible. But in abandoning the ocean, he stipulated for free permission to roam at large over the wide expanse of his native country, and in a few days after the intelligence had arrived of his father's death, he was seen leaving his native village with an elastic step, with a staff in his hand, and a small portmanteau under his arm.

Here I must leave my hero for the present, and ask the gentle reader to accompany me to the pleasant village of Carondelet, or, as it is more commonly called, Vide Poche, on the margin of the Mississippi. Although now dwindled into an obscure and ruinous hamlet, remarkable only for its outlandish huts and lean ponies, it was then the goodly seat of a prosperous community. It is situated on the western shore of the river, in a beautiful little amphitheatre, which seemed to have been scooped out for the very purpose. The banks of the Mississippi at this place are composed of a range of hills rising abruptly from the water's edge. The town occupies a sort of cove, formed by a small plat of table land, surrounded on three sides by hills. The houses occupy the whole of this little area, including the hill-sides; and are models of primitive rudeness, carelessness, and comfort. They were sometimes of stone; but usually of framed timber, with mud walls; and all the rooms being arranged on the ground floor, their circumference was often oddly disproportioned to their height. In a few of the better sort, spacious piazzas, formed by the projection of the roof, surrounded the buildings, giving to them both coolness and a remarkable air of comfort. The enormous steep roofs were often quadrangular, so as to form a point in the middle, surmounted by a ball, a weathercock, or a cross. Gardens, stocked with fruit trees and flowering shrubs, encompassed the dwellings, enclosed with rough stone walls, or stockades made by driving large stakes in the ground. The dwelling stood apart, having each its own little domain about it; and when it is added that the streets were narrow and irregular, it will be observed that the whole scene was odd and picturesque.

    The inhabitants presented, as I suppose, a fair specimen of the French peasantry, as they existed in France previous to the first revolution. They had all the levity, the kindness, and the contentment which are so well described by Sterne, with a simplicity which was perfectly childlike. Though subject at the date of our tale to a foreign king, they were as good republicans as if they had been trained up in one of our own colonies. They knew the restraints and distinctions of a monarchy only by report, practising the most rigid equality among themselves, and never troubling their heads to inquire how things were ordered elsewhere. The French commandants and priests, who ruled in their numerous colonies, had always the knack of giving a parental character to their sway, and governed with so much mildness, that the people never thought of questioning either the source or extent of their authority; while the English invariably alienate the affections of their colonists by oppression. The inhabitants of Vide Poche were all plebeians; a few who traded with the Indians had amassed some little property; the remainder were hunters and boatmen—men who traversed the great prairies of the West, and traced the largest rivers to their sources, fiddling and laughing all the way, lodging and smoking in the Indian wigwams, and never dreaming of fatigue or danger.

    To return to our story. It was a sultry afternoon in June. Not a breath of air was stirring—the intense glare of the sun had driven every animal to some shelter—the parched soil glowed with heat, and even the plants drooped. There was, however, a pleasant coolness and an inviting serenity among the dwellings of the French. The trees that stood thick around them threw a dense shade, which contrasted delightfully with the glaring fierceness of the sunbeams. The broad leaf of the catalpa and the rich green of the locust afforded relief to the eye; bowers of sweetbrier and honeysuckle, mingled with luxuriant clumps of the white and red rose, gave fragrance to the air, and a romantic beauty to the scene.

In the cool veranda of one of the largest of those dwellings, sat a round-faced, laughing Frenchman. Near him sat Madame, his wife, a dark-eyed, wrinkled, sprightly old lady; and at her side was a beautiful girl of seventeen, their only daughter. The worthy couple had that mahogany tinge of complexion which belongs to this region; as to the young lady, politeness compels me to describe her hue as a brunette—and a beautiful brunette it was—fading into snow-white upon her neck, and deepening into a rich damask on her round smooth cheek. The ladies were sewing; and the gentleman was puffing his pipe with the composure of a man who feels conscious that he has a right to smoke his own tobacco in his own house, and with the deliberation of one who is master of his own time.

While thus engaged, their attention was attracted by the apparition of a man leading a jaded horse along the street. The stranger was young and slender; his dress had once been genteel, but was much worn, and showed signs of recent exposure to the weather. The traveller himself was tanned and weather-beaten, his hair tangled, and his chin unshaved; while the sorry nag, which he led by the bridle, had just life enough left in him to limp upon three legs. Worn down with fatigue, and covered with sweat and dust, the new comer halted in the street, as if unable to proceed, and looked around in search of a public house. Of a boy, who passed along, he inquired for a tavern; but the lad, unable to understand him, shook his head. He put the same question to several others, with no better success; until Monsieur Dunois, the gentleman whom we have described above, seeing his embarrassment, stepped forward and invited him into his porch.

The stranger was no other than our friend Timothy Eleazer Tompkinson, who, in the course of a few months, had made his way from New England to Louisiana. It is unnecessary to recount the various expedients by which he maintained himself upon his journey. He was a lawyer, a doctor, or a mechanic, as occasion required. At one place, he pleaded a cause before a magistrate; at another, he drew a tooth; for one man he mended a lock; for another he set a timepiece; and by these and similar devices, he not only supported himself, but procured the means to purchase a horse, saddle, and bridle. Arrived at the frontier of Kentucky, his restless spirit still urged him forward, and he determined to strike across the wilderness to the French settlements, on the Mississippi. The distance was nearly three hundred miles, and the whole region through which he had to travel was uninhabited, except by Indians. Unaccustomed to the forest, he must have perished, had he not encountered a solitary hunter, who, pleased with his free and bold spirit, voluntarily conducted him throughout a considerable part of the route, taught him how to avoid the haunts of the savages, and instructed him in some of the arts of forest life. For the last two days he had wandered without food; and both himself and his horse were nearly exhausted when he reached the Mississippi, where some friendly Indians, of the Kaskaskia tribe, had ferried him across in their canoes. The arrival of a stranger at this secluded hamlet, by land, was quite an event, and little else was talked of, this evening, at the tea-tables of Carondelet.

M. Dunois, who had traded and travelled, valued himself highly on his knowledge of the English language, which he had attempted to teach to his daughter; and he no sooner discovered that this was the vernacular tongue of the stranger, than he opened a conversation in that dialect. The cork was drawn from a bottle of excellent claret, a pitcher of limpid water from the fountain was brought, and our hero having moistened his parched lips, and seated himself in the coolest veranda of Vide Poche, felt quite refreshed. The following dialogue then ensued:

"Pray, sir," said Timothy Eleazer, with his best college bow, "can you direct me to a tavern?"

"Tavern! *vat* you call? *eh?* Oh la! *d'auberge*—no, Monsieur, *dere* is no tavern *en Vide Poche.*"

"That is awkward enough—what shall I do? my horse must be fed, and I am almost starved."

"*Eh bien?* you will have some *ros bif,* and somebody for eat your *cheval! n'est ce pas?*"

"I need food and lodging, and know not where to go."

"*Fude! vat* is *fude,* Marie? Ah ha! *aliment. Sacre! Monsieur* is *hongry; Loge!* here is *ver* good place, *chez moi.* You shall stay *vid* me. *Ver* good *loge* here, and plenty for eat you, *et votre cheval.*"

Timothy "hoped he didn't intrude;" but a man who has been lost in the woods is not very apt to stand on ceremony; and as he glanced at the symptoms of plenty which surrounded him, at the good-humoured hostess, and at the fair Marie, a spectator would have judged that his fears of intrusion were overbalanced by feelings of self-gratulation at having fallen into the hands of such good Samaritans. He soon found that the hospitality of this worthy family was of the most substantial kind. In a moment his tired nag was led to the stable, and our hero, so lately a wanderer, found himself an honoured and cherished guest.

The air of Vide Poche agreed well with him. The free and social habits of the French were exactly to his taste. Although their pockets, as the name of their town implies, were not lined with gold, there was plenty in their dwellings and cheerfulness in their hearts.

He was delighted with the harmony and the apparent unity, both of feeling and interest, which bound this little community together. They were like a single family; their hearts beat in unison, "as the heart of one man." There was but one circle. Though some were poorer than others, they all mingled in the same dance; and as none claimed superiority, or attempted to put others to shame by affecting a show of wealth, there was little envy or malice. All were equally illiterate, with the exception of Mons. Dunois and the priest, who had travelled, and who spoke, the one Latin, and the other, as we have seen, English. But so far from assuming any airs on account of these attainments, they were the plainest and most sociable men in the village, and were reverenced as much for their benevolence as for their superior knowledge.

All this chimed so well with the feelings of Mr. Timothy Eleazer Tompkinson, that he resolved forthwith to engraft himself upon this cheerful and vigorous stock. The next thing was to choose a profession; but he had too much common sense to suffer so small a matter as this to cause him any embarrassment. I am not aware of the precise motive which determined him to embrace the practice of physic. It might have been benevolence, or a conviction of special vocation for the healing art; but I rather attribute it to a motive which I suspect too often allures our youth to become the disciples of Æsculapius, namely, the occult nature of the science, which enables an adroit practitioner to cover his ignorance so completely as to defy detection. Timothy had discovered that when he practised law, any spectator could expose the fallacy of his arguments; when he mended clocks, they often refused to go; but the case was different with his patients; if, in spite of his drugs, they refused *to go,* it was well for them and for him; and if they *did go,* nobody knew whom to blame. To say the truth, he never presumed to "exhibit" any drug more active than charcoal, brickdust, or flour; and his success had heretofore been quite marvellous.

He therefore took the earliest opportunity of disclosing to his host that he was a physician, and was disposed to exercise his calling for the benefit of the good people of Carondelet.

"*Eh bien!*" exclaimed M. Dunois, "*un medecin! ver* good; *ver mosh* fine *ting* for Vide Poche; *vat* can you cure?"

"Oh, I am not particular; I can cure one thing almost as well as another."

"You can cure every *ting, eh?—de fevre, de break-bone, de catch-cold—dat* is fine *ting,* you shall stay *chez Vide Poche.*"

So the question was settled.

Had there been a newspaper in Carondelet, the name of Doctor Timothy Eleazer Tompkinson, "from the United States," would, doubtless, have figured in its columns. But as there was no such thing, our hero resorted to other means of acquiring notoriety. In the first place, having procured a suitable cabin, the whole village was searched for vials, and gallipots, and little boxes, and big bottles, which, being filled with liquids and unguents of various hues, were "wisely set for show," at the window. But the greatest affair of all was a certain machine, for the invention of which Doctor Tompkinson ought to have had a patent. This was no other than a wheel, turning on an axis, and surrounded by an immovable rim, within which it revolved. Upon the wheel Timothy wrote the name of every disease which he could recollect, as well as every dreadful accident to which flesh is heir; and on the rim he inscribed the cures. When the remedy for any disorder was required, the wheel was set in motion, and on its stopping, the cure was found opposite the disease. The honest villagers crowded to see "the magic wheel," and vied in their courtesies to its fortunate possessor, who was rising fast into celebrity, when his prospects were clouded by an untoward event.

In the midst of the village stood the chapel—a low, oblong building, whose gable end was presented to the street, and behind which was a cemetery, where all the graves were marked by great wooden crosses, instead of tombstones. Here the good Catholics repaired every morning and evening to perform their devotions, and confess their peccadilloes to the priest. Hither one morning, at an earlier hour than usual, was seen repairing the fair Marie Dunois, with a step as light as the zephyr and a face radiant as the dawn. Kneeling beside the worthy old man, who placed his withered hand upon her raven locks, she began in a low, earnest tone to unburthen her mind. Suddenly the ecclesiastic started from his seat, exclaiming,

"Ah, the insolent! how did he dare to make such an avowal?"

"He meant no harm, I assure you, father," replied Marie.

"How do you know that?"

"He told me so, with his own mouth. He said that he valued my happiness more than his own; and that he would rather swallow all the physic in his shop, than offend me."

"Very pretty talk, truly! Do you not know that he is a heretic, and that no reliance can be placed in him?"

"Very true, Father Augustin, but then he is so agreeable."

"Besides, he is a Yankee; and does not understand your language."

"Oh, I understand him very well; and he says he will teach me to speak English. Don't you think him very handsome, Father Augustin?"

"I am afraid, my child, that this adventurer has imposed too much upon your youth and innocence."

"No, indeed, Father Augustin, I am old enough to know when a gentleman is sincere, and all that. Don't you think Doctor Tompkinson plays beautifully on the flute? and on the violin, he plays almost as well as you, father."

"Pshaw! go, go, I shall inform your parents."

"Oh dear, I have no objections to that; they will feel highly honoured by Doctor Tompkinson's partiality for me."

Nevertheless the pretty Marie blushed and cast down her eyes when she met her father at breakfast that morning, and no sooner was that meal despatched than she hastened to her own room. Presently came Father Augustin, and after an hour's conference, Monsieur Dunois, evidently much agitated, sallied forth in search of our hero.

"*Vel, sair!*" he exclaimed as they met, "I *ave* found you out! I *ave catch de Yankee!*"

"How?"

"How! you *ave* court my daughter; *dat is how! sacre!* you *ave* make love *avec ma Marie, dat* is how enough, *Monsieur docteur.*"

"My dear sir, pray be composed, there is some mistake."

"*Dere* is no mistake. I *vill* not be *compose*—I *will* not be *impose, too! diable!* Suppose some *gentilhomme* court *ma Marie contrair* to my *vish*, shall I sit down *compose?*"

"Really, sir, I see no reason for this passion," replied the cautious

Timothy, who saw his advantage in keeping cool.

"Sair, I ave raison," exclaimed the enraged Frenchman; "I *ave too mosch raison. Vous etez traitre!* you are *de* sly *dem* rogue! You very pretty *docteur!* very *ansome* Yankee *docteur!* can you no mix *de physique,* and draw *de* blood, *vidout* make love *avec* all *the French gal?"*

"I assure you, sir, the ladies have misconstrued something that I have said merely in jest—"

"*Jest! vat* is *jest? ah ha! raillerie; fon—vat, sair,* you court *ma fille* for *fon?* very *ansome fon!* you make love *avec de* French *gal* for *fon, eh?* Suppose *bam bye* you marry some of *dem* for *fon! diable!* Suppose, maybe, I break all your bone, for *fon, vid* my *cane, eh,* how you like him?"

"My dear sir, if you will tell me coolly what you complain of, I will endeavour to explain."

"*Sair,* I complain for many *ting.* I sorry for you make love *avec ma fille, vidout* my leave—*dat* is *von ting;* I very *mosch incense* for you court *ma chile* for *fon—dat* is *nodder ting;* den I *ave raison* to be *fache* for you *faire la cour a* two, *tree* lady all same *tem.*"

The last of these accusations was unjust. Timothy had not really intended to pay his devotions to more than one lady. But the females all admired him, and in their confidential conversations with the priest, who was no great connoisseur in the affairs of the heart, spoke of him in such high terms of approbation, as to induce the holy man to believe that he was actually playing the coquette. What Monsieur Dunois and the priest believed, soon became the belief of the village; and the men all condemned, while the ladies sympathized with, the ingenious stranger. The doctor, of course, changed his lodging; and ceased to have any intercourse with Mademoiselle Dunois, except by means of expressive glances and significant pressures of the hand as they met in the dances, which occurred almost every evening.

Things now looked gloomy; our friend Timothy lost his practice; and a fortunate circumstance it was for him, as well as for those who might otherwise have been his patients. He now had leisure to make hunting excursions, and expeditions upon the water; and his skill in the management of a boat, as well as his courage and address in every emergency, soon gained him friends. His vivacity, his versatility and promptness, won daily upon his comrades; he became a daring hunter, a skilful woodsman, and a favourite of all the young men of the village.

Such was the posture of affairs, and Doctor Tompkinson was sitting one evening in his lonely room, *quite out of patients,* as a punster would

A Legend of Carondelet.   73

say, when he was called in haste to visit a young lady who had met with the misfortune of having a fish-bone stuck in her throat. The priest had exercised all his skill—the old ladies had exhausted their recipes without effect; and, as a last resort, it was determined to consult Dr. Tompkinson and the magic wheel. Our hero, with great alacrity, brushed the dust from the neglected machine, set it in motion, and waited patiently until it stopped, when opposite to the word "choking" was found "bleeding." The doctor, somewhat perplexed, repeated the experiment; but, the result being the same, resolved to obey the oracle, and trust to fortune. Having prepared his bandages and lancet, he repaired to the sufferer, who, opening her eyes and beholding the operator brandishing a bright instrument, and naturally supposing that the part affected would be the first point of attack, and that her throat would be cut from ear to ear, uttered a terrific scream, and—out flew the bone! "St. Anthony! what a miraculous cure!" exclaimed the priest.

"Ste. Genevieve! what a noble physician!" cried all the ladies.

And the whole village of Vide Poche was alive with wonder and loud in praise of the consummate sagacity of the young American. Never did a man rise so suddenly to the highest pinnacle of public favour—never did Doctor Tompkinson shake so many hard hands, or receive so many bright smiles and courtesies, as on this evening. The news soon flew to the tea-table of Monsieur Dunois, who had already begun to repent of his harshness to our hero, and whose ardent feelings, easily excited, now prompted him into the opposite extreme. Seeing the object of his solicitude passing his door, while the first gush of returning kindness was flowing through his heart, he rushed out and caught him in his arms. "*Ah, mon ami!*" exclaimed he, "I *ave* been *mistake!* I *ave* been *impose!* you are *de grand medecin!* you shall marry *avec* my *gal!*" and without waiting for any reply, he dragged him into the house.

Shortly after this event, the smartest and merriest wedding that ever was seen in Carondelet was celebrated under the hospitable roof of Monsieur Dunois, and our hero became the happy husband of the beautiful and artless Marie. On that night, every fiddle and every foot in Vide Poche did its duty; even the priest wore his best robes and kindest smile at the marriage feast of the lucky heretic. Mr. Tompkinson immediately abandoned the practice of physic; the magic wheel disappeared; and he embarked in business as an Indian trader. Here his genius found an appropriate field. With his band of adventurous boatmen he navigated the long rivers of the West to their tributary fountains; he visited the wigwams of tribes afar off, to whom the white man was not yet known as a scourge; he chased the buffalo over plains until then untrodden by any human foot but that of the savage, and returned laden with honest spoil. Year after year he pursued this toilsome traffic; until, having earned a competency, he sat down contented, and waxed as fat, as lazy, and as garrulous as any of his townsmen. He grew as swarthy as his neighbours, and as he wore a *capot* and smoked a short pipe, no one would have suspected that he was not a native, had it not been for his aunt, the worthy Miss Fidelity Tompkinson, who occupied the best room in his mansion, and who resolutely refused, through life, to eat *gumbo*-soup, to speak French, or to pay any reverence to that respectable man, the priest.

MICHEL DE COUCY.

On a pleasant day in September, 1750, two horsemen were seen slowly winding their way along the road leading by the margin of the Mississippi river, from the French village of *Notre Dame de Kaskaskia*, to Fort Chartres. One of them, who appeared to be about forty years of age, was a man of gay and martial appearance. He wore an elegant military undress, and rode gracefully on a fine and high-mettled horse. He was the commandant of Fort Chartres, and in virtue of that office, governor of the French settlements in Illinois, which he ruled with a power little less than despotic, but with a mildness that savoured more of parental than of sovereign authority. His companion was the superior of the convent of Jesuits at Kaskaskia, of whose personal appearance we have no accurate account; but we suppose that he was a tall, lank, homely man, with a cunning, mysterious, austere look, such as monks and superiors of convents usually wear on public occasions, and who, while he ruled his own little community with a high hand, acquired considerable influence in the affairs of the colony by his deferential deportment towards the commander of his majesty's forces. The riders were followed by a small train, which seemed to be paraded rather for show than for protection, consisting of half a dozen gaudily dressed huzzars, mounted on the small fiery horses of the country, which, having run wild in their early years, retained ever after their original impatience of restraint.

Their way led through that beautiful plain which is now called the American bottom, an extensive tract of rich, flat, alluvial soil, which lies along the eastern shore of the Mississippi and Illinois, and reaches from the river to the bluffs, and which is justly regarded as containing the greatest body of fertile land in this country, or perhaps in the universe. Part of this plain is covered with timber, the remainder is open prairie, and the whole interspersed with groves of vine and native fruit. Here are to be seen the indigenous productions of this climate in the greatest variety and highest perfection. The tallest cotton-wood and sycamore trees, which rear their enormous shafts to an amazing height, are covered with vines equally aspiring, while the thickets are matted together with smaller vines, and loaded with innumerable clusters of fine grapes. Our travellers beheld groves of the wild apple, whose blossoms in the spring season fill the air of this region with a delightful fragrance, and whose limbs were now bending under loads of useless fruit. They saw hundreds of acres covered with the wild plumb, of which there are many varieties, deepening in colour from a light yellow to a deep crimson, and the ripe fruit of which now hung in amazing quantities, and in appearance rich and beautiful beyond description. The walnut, the peccan, and other fine nuts abounded, the whole combining with the remarkable beauty of the autumn sky in this country, and the serenity and mildness of the atmosphere, to fill the mind with ideas of luxury and plenty.

  The plain, which at some places spreads out to the breadth of twelve miles, was confined to a narrow strip, at the point now travelled by the riders whom we have described, and their path, which sometimes approached the river, at others wound along the foot of the bluffs, a ridge of abrupt hills rising perpendicularly to the height of more than a hundred feet, and supposed to have been anciently washed by the Mississippi. Advancing into the Prairie de Rocher, they beheld an open plain, bounded on one side by the river, and on the other by a tall barrier of solid rock, whose summit projects over its base, and whose highest points, which are beautifully rounded, are covered with rich soil and prairie grass, and here and there ornamented with a single tree. At the foot of this rock, and extending thence to the river, was a large village, called, in reference to its situation, the village of Prairie de Rocher. Adjoining this was a large enclosure called the "Common Field," which was held in severalty by the inhabitants, each of whom owned a greater or less number of acres, according to his ability, and the whole of which was surrounded by a common fence without partitions. Each person cultivated his own part, and had a right to pasturage at proper seasons in proportion to the quantity of his land; and the whole business of fencing, tilling, and pasturing, was regulated by village ordinances, and conducted with a harmony which is not known to have existed in any other community similarly situated. Lots in the "Common Field" were held by purchase or grant from the French crown, the rest of the ground in and around the village was held by the inhabitants *in common,* and portions of it were reduced to private property by a simple procedure. When a young man married, or a person wished *to settle* in the village, an instrument of writing was drawn and signed by all the inhabitants, vesting in him the fee-simple of a lot for building, and equal rights with the others in their common property. But we detain the reader too long from the gay and gentle company who were about to honour the rustic villagers with their august presence.

They had passed the Common Field, now covered with a ripening crop of Indian corn, and were entering the village when their attention was attracted by a crowd of persons assembled in front of the cottage of Michel de Coucy. Honest Michel himself, who when at home usually sat under a spreading catalpa before his own door, with a red cap on his head, and a short black pipe in his mouth, the very emblem of content and placid composure, now stood in the midst of the concourse, weeping, raving, and threatening, with the most vehement gestures. He was a small, thin, dark man, with black hair, and an eye that he might have been suspected of inheriting from the aborigines, had not his character been so genuinely French as fully to redeem the purity of descent. He was as honest as gay, and as contented a soul as ever breathed, famed for the simplicity and benevolence of his character, as well as for a vein of humour, which rendered him at all times an agreeable companion. In fact, to smoke his pipe, to do kind actions, and to tell pleasant tales and sly jests, seemed to be the business of his life, his other occupations being of secondary importance. Born in the wilds of Canada, and reared in the woods and upon the water, he was equally at home, whether paddling his canoe to the sources of our largest rivers, or wandering alone through the trackless forest. After his emigration to the borders of the Mississippi, his chief occupation became that of a boatman, and none pulled a better oar or sung with truer cadence the animating notes of the boat song than Michel de Coucy. The Canadian boatmen are the hardiest and merriest of men; if their boat is stranded they plunge into the water in all weathers, diving and swimming about as if in their native element; if it storms, they sleep or revel under the protection of a high bank, and whether pulling down the stream, or pushing laboriously against it, the shores ring with their voices. One will recount his adventures, another will imitate the Indian yell, the roar of the alligator, the hissing of the snake, or the chattering of the paroquet; and anon the whole will chant their rude ditties concerning the dangers of rapids, snags, and sawyers, or the pleasures of home, the vintage, and the dance. Michel was an adept at all these things, and he loved them as a Cossack loves plunder, or a Dutchman hard work and money. He was the darling of the crew, for he could skin a deer, cook a fish, scrape a chin or a fiddle with equal adroitness, and always performed such offices so good-humouredly, that his companions, in compliment to his universal genius, kept it in continual employment. When the boat was in motion he was always tugging at the oar or the fiddle-bow, when it landed, and the crew sat round their camp fire, he cooked, sung, and told merry stories; on Sunday he shaved the whole company, even at the risk of neglecting his own visage, and was after all the merriest and most respectable man in the boat. With all this, Michel was temperate and careful of his earnings, which he shrewdly husbanded in a leathern purse during every voyage, and handed over on his return to his wife, who hid them under the floor of their cabin. Such talents could not fail to bring honour and promotion to their possessor; Michel became popular among his comrades, and having acquired experience in his craft, in a few years rose to the charge of a boat and the title of captain.

Having acquired a decent competency by the time he reached the meridian of life, Michel thought it expedient, and his wife thought so too, that he should consult his own comfort for the rest of his days. He therefore abandoned his frail cabin, which in truth was beginning to stumble about his ears, and built a goodly house with substantial mud walls, surrounded on all sides by cool piazzas, and planted his yard full of catalpas and black locusts. He purchased a large lot in the common field, and took unto himself herds of black cattle and droves of French ponies.

Michel, however, still loved the water, and like a sprightly spaniel, could be induced to leap into it upon the slightest invitation. He continued to make a voyage of three or four months annually, and spent the remainder of his time in cultivating his crop, smoking his pipe, attending the king-balls, and playing the fiddle. He had his crosses like other men: his chimney often smoked, and Madame Felicité, his wife, sometimes got out of temper; his cattle occasionally had the murrain, the frost nipped his corn, and more than once he lost both boat and cargo by running on the snags and sawyers of the Mississippi. But none of these things ever disturbed the placid spirit of Michel; a single shrug, and a "*Sacre!*" were the strongest symptoms of emotion which ever were elicited from him by such disasters, and he would most frequently smile, and exclaim in the moment of misfortune, "*C'est toute le même chose.*" It is said that he could even bear the breaking of a fiddle-string, a lecture from his wife, or a public admonition from the priest for not going to confession, with the same composure which he preserved on less provoking occasions. He had his joys, too, and these greatly predominated. His wife was an excellent manager, made charming *gumbo soup,* and could interpret dreams; his daughter, Genevieve, was as fair as the swans that sailed on the Mississippi; and his neighbours loved him. He was head man at the balls; for as they had no hireling fiddlers in those days, the honourable office of musician was filled in turn by such heads of families as were blessed with musical ears and limber elbows; and none touched the violin so cleverly as Michel, who continually cheered the dancers with his voice, as he kept time with head and feet. Happy days of equality and glee! when every man who owned a cabin, a car, and a pony was a French gentleman, when the evening gun of the fort and the matin bell of the chapel were daily heard; and the song and dance prevailed, wherever a plank floor, a French girl, and a fiddle could be paraded.

Such being the character and standing of worthy Michel de Coucy, it is not surprising that the whole village of Prairie de Rocher should have been astonished at beholding him in the attitudes of rage and grief, swearing and wailing, and beating the air with his clenched fists; nor that even such august personages, as the commandant of Fort Chartres and the superior of the Jesuits at Notre Dame de Kaskaskia, should marvel thereat. Nor was Michel a man whose sorrows would be slightly viewed by his neighbours; he had as large a house, as much land, and as many horned brutes and ponies as the best of them; and a man in easy circumstances is always sure of sympathy when in trouble. Michel, moreover, was popular; and when the voice of distress issued from his cottage, every one ran to condole with him; even the commandant and the superior of the Jesuits felt it incumbent on them to rein up their steeds and inquire the cause of this unusual disturbance.

It seems that Michel having been many years employed as a carrier of merchandise for others, began at last to think that he might as well freight his boat upon his own account; and had for the last two or three years dabbled pretty extensively in the ticklish business of buying and selling. The long-cherished hoard of Spanish dollars, which his wife had buried under the cabin-floor, had been transferred, when he removed to his new house, to a similar place of deposit, a plank having been left unfastened for that express purpose. But when he embarked in traffic, those silver coins were exchanged for furs, the furs for goods, wares, and merchandise, and the latter for notes of hand and fair promises. Still Michel and his wife were content; for the nominal sum secured by fair words and due-bills trebled the actual amount that had been disbursed in hard money, and they doubted not that it would all come in, in due time. But in the mean while he had entered into some pecuniary engagements which could be discharged only with cash, and found himself in an embarrassing situation. He had never before owed money, and had now to face a creditor for the first time! In this dilemma, being unwilling to publish his situation to his own neighbours, he bethought himself of a certain Pedro Garcia, a Spaniard, who lived on the opposite side of the river, in a wilderness track of broken country, where no law was known, and where the military arm of the French authority could scarcely reach him. This Pedro was a black-whiskered, ill-looking fellow, who had amassed a large fortune, nobody knew how. He had a farm, and a good many slaves; he traded with the Indians, who hated him, and went often to New Orleans, were he lost and won large sums by gambling, and was more than once in the hands of the police. Nobody liked Pedro; the French had little to say to him, and the Indians looked with distrust at the long dirk which he carried rather ostentatiously in his bosom. But Michel wanted money, and Pedro had it, and without more ado, the distressed Frenchman applied to the Spaniard for a loan. Pedro, who knew that Michel was abundantly able to repay him, and saw that he was only hard pressed at the moment, in consequence of his reluctance to call upon those who owed him, readily advanced the sum required, taking Michel's bond for the amount, payable at the end of six months, with usury.

The six months soon rolled round, and Michel was not prepared to pay his bond. He had waited from day to day in the vain hope that his debtors would discharge their dues; and at last finding that they did not come forward voluntarily, he deferred from hour to hour the disagreeable task of dunning them, because it was so abhorrent to his feelings, that he could not muster sufficient resolution to undertake it. The day of payment came, and with it came Pedro Garcia, and Michel was constrained to acknowledge that he could not fulfil his engagement. Garcia knit his black brows and swore like a trooper, and although his debtor spoke fairly and humbly, and made liberal propositions, the relentless creditor would take nothing but his money, and forthwith hied to the civil magistrate of the village. The minister of the law heard the application with surprise, and expressed in emphatic language his astonishment that a subject of Spain should think of suing a subject of the Grand Monarque, within the territory of France, and above all that he should have the assurance to propose to employ an officer of the French crown, in so flagrant an act of contumacy. "The laws of France," said this worthy functionary, "are made for the benefit of the French people and the honour of their king, and not for Spaniards, and my duty is to administer those laws to my fellow-subjects, not to foreigners. Go, you are not under my jurisdiction—I know nothing of you,—and am only in doubt whether your attempt to employ the laws of my country against a Frenchman is not a high misdemeanour."

Pedro, finding that he could obtain no satisfaction from the civil authority, determined to resort to the military, and as the commandant was absent, laid the matter before his lieutenant. This gentleman called to his assistance the chaplain, a very worthy priest, who having been long attached to the army, was experienced in questions of *meum* and *tuum*, and being thus fortified, proceeded to hear the complaint, and examine the papers of Pedro Garcia.

"*Ma foi!*" what is this?" exclaimed Captain de la Val, as he glanced his eye over the unlucky instrument of writing, laid before him by the Spaniard.

"It is Michel de Coucy's bond, for the sum I loaned him," replied the plaintiff.

"*Diable!* how shall I know this to be a bond, seeing that it is written in an unknown tongue?"

"It is Spanish, a language which your excellency no doubt speaks with the elegance and propriety of a native Castilian."

"You do my excellency unmerited honour, and must permit me to inform you, that *officially* I am not to be presumed to know any other language than my own."

"The purport of the instrument," said Garcia, "may readily be ascertained by means of an interpreter."

"Indeed!" exclaimed the officer, "can you not also provide a deputy-commanding officer to perform the rest of my duty? If I must read your papers by proxy, I may as well decide in the same way."

"Captain de la Val," said the priest, "takes a very proper and nice distinction. The first step in the adjustment of a controversy is to ascertain the true intent and meaning of the contract between the parties litigant, and it would ill become the dignity of any high tribunal to entrust the decision of that important point to an irresponsible agent."

"What shall I do?" inquired the alarmed money-lender.

"That I cannot tell," replied the officer; "of this, however, I am clear, that a paper written in Spanish can be of no validity in a French court, for there would be an obvious absurdity in requiring the ministers of justice, whether civil or military, to decide on that which they cannot read."

"Besides," said the priest, who began to envy the wisdom of the captain, "his most Christian Majesty has appointed notaries whose business it is to draw such writings between parties, and as this paper was not drawn by a proper notarial scribe, we cannot know whether it is in due form of law."

"What matters it about form," said the Spaniard, "if the writing contains a substantial promise?"

"My son," replied the chaplain, "you do not understand these matters. If a man makes a verbal engagement, the form thereof is not material, because in that case the creditor trusts to the honour and honesty of the debtor, and the latter is bound in conscience not to abuse that confidence; but if the parties reduce their contract to writing, the creditor reposes his trust, not in the virtue of the other party, but in the binding operations of the law, and if the work of the law is not made secure, the creditor must lose thereby, for he looked to that only for his payment."

"My bond is sufficient in law," contended Pedro; "it is in the form used by our Spanish notaries."

"Worse and worse," exclaimed the priest; "if his excellency the commanding officer should undertake to decide upon the validity of a writing authenticated by a Spanish functionary, it would doubtless be considered by his most Catholic Majesty as a very indelicate interference, inasmuch as he would be enforced, not only to weigh the language and construe the laws of Spain, but to look into the acts of the civil magistrates of that nation; and the consequence might be a war between two Christian princes."

Pedro Garcia, though he could not comprehend how the settling of a dispute between himself and Michel de Coucy could become the cause of war between two European kings, began to think that possibly he had mistaken his remedy, and making a sulky bow was about to retire, when Captain de la Val called him back and said,

"Senor Garcia, it is well known that Michel is no scholar, how then could he execute that bond?"

"He has made his mark," replied the other, showing the cross at the foot of the bond.

"Aha! but that same cross might stand with equal propriety for the name of any Catholic in Christendom."

"But I can prove by the notary that Michel made it."

"Like enough; but Michel does not understand Spanish, how then could he know the contents of that paper?"

"It was interpreted to him."

"But how can I know that it was interpreted correctly? In short," continued the officer, "I am induced to believe that this document is a forgery, and that it is my duty to lodge you in the guard chamber, until the return of the commandant."

"And if it be a forgery," added the priest, "there is little doubt in my mind that the counterfeiting the sign of the cross is an offence against our holy church, and of much higher grade than a common forgery."

Pedro, finding that the aspect of his case grew darker every moment, and fearing that he might be in the end handed over to the inquisition, began to supplicate for mercy, and being permitted to retire, hastily made good his retreat, marvelling at the strange turn in his affairs, which, from a simple creditor of Michel de Coucy, had converted him into an enemy of his Holiness the Pope and his most Christian Majesty the King of France.

Michel, who, when he saw Pedro take the road to Fort Chartes, had suspected his business, and hastily followed him, entered the quarters of Captain de la Val during the conference above described; and standing respectfully with his cap in his right hand, his left stuck in his waistband, and his mouth wide open, listened in mute admiration of the wisdom and nice sense of justice displayed by the priest and officer. As Pedro retired, he slipped after him, and, tapping him on the shoulder as he passed out of the main gate, said triumphantly, "*Bon jour,* Senor Garcia, your bond is too small—it will not cover the sore place! it is not worth a sous! Now come to my house when you get in a good humour and I will make a new bargain to pay you all I owe, and give you the word of honour of a French gentleman, which, Father Felix says, is better than a Spanish bond." Pedro paused a moment and laid his hand on his dirk—then turned on his heel and retired, without deigning to reply.

When he reached home he was half inclined to turn back and embrace

Michel's offer, but still believing that a bond, good or bad, was better than any parol engagement, he hastened to his friend the notary, on his own side of the river, and having informed him of all that had passed, requested him, when Michel should next cross into their territory, to have him arrested for his debt. To his surprise, the notary declined interfering in the business, highly extolling the good sense and courtesy displayed by the French functionaries, and declaring that he knew no law under which a Spaniard could sue a Frenchman, and that at all events it was extremely proper and decorous that the officers of France should abstain from meddling in matters of such high import, which ought to be left to ministers plenipotentiary, or to the crowned heads themselves.

"Then the long and short of the matter is," said Pedro, as he retired, "that I am to be cheated out of my money;" and he forthwith prayed to all the saints of whom he had any knowledge, to visit with special maledictions, the heads of Michel de Coucy, Chevalier Jean Philippe de la Val, Father Felix the priest, and all others directly or indirectly concerned in preventing him from recovering the amount nominated in his bond, with interest thereon, at the rate of ten per cent. per annum until paid.

People who live on the frontier imbibe very accurate notions of justice, and adopt summary modes of obtaining it; and Senor Pedro Garcia, not being a man to sit down quietly after a loss, and finding the door of the law closed against him, began to cast about for some other remedy. After brooding over the matter for several days, he at length devised a plan; and getting into his canoe in the night, paddled secretly over to the Illinois shore, where he remained concealed in a thicket, until Genevieve, the daughter of Michel, passing that way alone, he sallied out, and making her his prisoner, carried her off, leaving a placard in these words, "Meshell Coosy! French rascal! pay me my money, and you shall have your daughter!" Genevieve was a beautiful child of twelve years of age, the pride of the village, and the darling of her parents. She had seen Pedro before, and always with repulsive feelings; and when she found herself rudely seized by him, sued piteously for mercy, believing that he would sell her to the Sioux, the English, or the Long Knives, "of whom by parcels she had something heard,"—or to some other outlandish people, to be eaten at a great war-feast. Pedro, without regarding her cries, bore her to a secluded place, among the broken hills, and, summoning a score of his associates and dependents, prepared to make a stout resistance in case of pursuit.

When Michel discovered the outrage committed against him, in the person of his child, on whom he doated, he was inconsolable; not only were his parental feelings awakened, but his sense of honour was touched to the quick. He wept, raved, swore strange oaths, and vowed bitter vengeance. All who were acquainted with him knew that, gentle as he was, he was brave; he had been accustomed to face danger from his childhood; and when they heard the deep imprecations which he now poured forth, they were satisfied that Pedro would pay dearly for the cruel insult he had perpetrated. The whole male population of the village immediately volunteered to accompany him to the rescue; and the distressed father, after thanking them with tears of gratitude, urged them to arm themselves without delay. It was at this juncture that the commandant and the superior of the Jesuits opportunely arrived, and having heard of the circumstances, Michel was enjoined to proceed no further in his plan of revenge, the commandant promising to take immediate measures for the restoration of his daughter.

Michel, who, believing that in wisdom, power, and goodness the commandant was second only to the king, was greatly composed by this assurance, and although his fellow-villagers continued to be ripe for an immediate inroad into the wilderness where Pedro lurked, he restrained their ardour, and passed the night in more tranquility than could have been expected. Early on the following morning he received a summons to attend the commandant at Fort Chartres, which was distant two miles from the village; and set out, with Madame Felicité, in one of those commodious vehicles, half-chaise and half-cart, which were fashionable among the Canadian French of those days, and are still to be seen in daily use among their descendants, at the famous village of *Vide Poche,* otherwise called Carondelet, in Missouri.

Fort Chartres was at that time the largest and most extensive fortification owned by the French in America, and was the seat of government for all their settlements in Illinois. Its shape was a regular quadrangle, with bastions at the angles, the sides of the exterior polygon being four hundred and ninety feet in extent; and the walls, which were two feet and two inches thick and twelve feet high, were built of stone, and plastered over. It was pierced all round, at regular distances, with loopholes for musketry, and had two port-holes for cannon in each face, and two in the flanks of each bastion. If any of my fair readers, who are desirous to know the exact description of this celebrated fortress, should be anxious to ascertain what is meant by "an irregular quadrangle with bastions at the angles," I am happy to inform them that they may obtain an exact idea of the figure intended to be described, by laying on the table before them an old-fashioned square pincushion, of which one side is a little longer than the other three, with large tassels at the corners. Such was precisely the shape of Fort Chartres. Within the walls were extensive buildings of stone, for the accommodation of the garrison:—a fine house for the commandant, quarters for the officers, and barracks for the soldiers, together with a great magazine, a chapel, and a snug cell for the priest, who officiated here, and at the village of Fort Chartres adjacent. This was the strong hold of power and the seat of festivity; here, on all suitable occasions, were assembled the rank, beauty, and fashion of the colony; and here could be paraded as many handsome French girls as one could wish to behold.

Michel entered the main gate of the fort, with a countenance of sorrow, far different from his usual gaiety, when he came to head-quarters an invited guest; and his feelings could be with difficulty restrained when he beheld the dark visage of Pedro Garcia. The latter had been induced to give his attendance by a missive from the commandant, assuring him of a safe-conduct to and from the fort, and that all amicable means would be used to settle the unfortunate difference between Michel and himself. Being naturally bold and impudent, and finding, too, that the delicate little Genevieve was withering like a plucked flower, and was at best a troublesome guest,—he came at the summons, and stood confronted with the incensed Frenchman. There, too, came all the relations of Michel and Felicité, and divers other of the villagers, burning with indignation—there stood Captain de la Val, Father Felix, the magistrate, and the notary, as dignified and complacent as if nothing had happened—and there sat several aged chiefs of the Kaskaskia tribe, in grave and solemn expectation, wondering at the levity of the whites, who could hold a counsel on a matter of such high import, without making presents, tendering the wampum, and smoking the great pipe.

The commandant examined the bond, heard the evidence and the decisions of his lieutenant, and of the civil officers on both sides of the river. He pronounced the conduct of all the functionaries, civil and military, to have been highly decorous and proper, and hoped that, in future, no Spaniard would presume to sue a Frenchman without his leave first had and obtained. He censured Pedro for the violent capture of the innocent Genevieve, and finally decreed that the latter should be safely returned to her parents, that Michel should pay to Pedro the principal borrowed without interest, the latter being withheld as a fine for the violence committed in the French territory, and that both the parties litigant should stand committed until this sentence should be fully complied with. Pedro remonstrated against the latter part of the decree, as a breach of his safe-conduct, but the commandant decided that he had guaranteed his safety in *going* and *coming,* but he had not precluded himself from fixing the length of time during which he should have the pleasure of Senor Garcia's company. The latter, finding himself entrapped, made a merit of necessity, and despatched an order for the little Genevieve, who was soon given to her parents' arms.

We cannot describe their joy, nor the spontaneous burst of sympathy which ran through the assembly, when the lost child was restored. The Indians, who had sat motionless as statues throughout the whole scene, preserving an inflexibility of muscle which nothing could change, rose when they beheld this affecting meeting, and said to each other, "Very good." One of them then stepped forward, and addressing the commandant, said, "Father, we came to see you do justice; we opened our ears, and our hearts are satisfied. The cunning black serpent crawled into the nest of the turtle, and stole away the young dove; but our father is an eagle, very strong and brave; he is wiser than the serpent; he has brought back the young dove, and the old turtles sing with joy. Father, we are satisfied, it is all very good. We bid you farewell." Then advancing to the commandant, each of the chiefs gave his right hand, and stalked out of the audience chamber, without deigning to notice any other person.

As for Michel, he had now no difficulty in paying his debt; for those who owed him, when they found that his misfortune had grown out of their own delinquency, immediately raised among them the sum required; and Michel retired well satisfied, but convinced of three truths, which he continued to maintain through life: first, that French laws surpass all others in wisdom and justice; second, that Spaniards with black whiskers are not to be trusted; and third, that it is safer to bury money under the floor than to embark it in traffic; and he thereupon made a vow to his patron saint, that whenever the leathern bag should be replenished, it should be restored to a place of deposit, there to remain as a talisman against the like misfortune in future.

NOTE.—This tale was suggested by an incident which really occurred in the early history of the French settlements in Illinois. A lady was still living there, a few years ago, who had been captured when a child by a creditor of her father, and carried to the opposite side of the river, where she was detained until the debt was arranged. Although the country on both sides of the river was under the same jurisdiction, some amusing negotiations took place, in consequence of the ignorance of the parties of that fact and of their respective rights. In our picture, the French officers are supposed to have humoured the mistake for the joke of the thing, as well as for the sake of rescuing the child from durance. There were no newspapers in those days, and the schoolmaster was not abroad, wherefore honest Michel and his friends may be pardoned for supposing that the King of Spain ruled the western side of the Mississippi.

THE SILVER MINE.
A TALE OF MISSOURI.

Some twelve or thirteen years ago, when the good land on the northern frontier of Missouri was beginning to be found out, and the village of Palmyra had been recently *located* on the extreme verge of the settlements of the white men, uncle Moses, who had built his cabin hard by, went into that promising village one day, in hopes of finding a letter from his cousin David, then at Louisville. and to whom he had written to come to Missouri. Three hours' pleasant ride brought him *to town*. He soon found Major Obadiah——, who had been lately appointed postmaster, and who had such an aversion to confinement, that he appropriated his hat to all the purposes of a post-office—an arrangement by which he complied with the law, requiring him to take special care of all letters and papers committed to his keeping, and the instructions directing him to be always found *in* his office, and, at the same time, enjoyed such locomotive freedom, as permitted him to go hunting or fishing, at his pleasure. He was thus ready at all times, wherever he might be, to answer any call on his department, promptly.

The major, seating himself on the grass, emptied his hat of its contents, and requested uncle Moses to assist him in hunting for his letter: "whenever you come to any that looks dirty and greasy, like these," said he, "just throw them in that pile; they are all *dead* letters, and I intend to send them off to head quarters, the very next time the post rider comes, for I can't afford to *tote* them any longer, encumbering up *the office* for nothing." Uncle Moses thought that they were at *head* quarters already, but made no remark, and quietly putting on his spectacles, gave his assistance as required.

After a quarter of an hour's careful examination, it was agreed by both, that there was no letter *in the office* for uncle Moses.

"But stop," said the postmaster, as uncle Moses was preparing to mount his horse, "you are a trading character, come let me sell you a lot of goods at wholesale. Willy Wan, the owner, has gone to St. Louis to lay in a fresh supply, and has left me to keep store for him 'til he returns. He had almost sold out, and I hate to be cramped up in a house all day, so I have packed up the whole stock in these two bundles"—hauling them out of his coat pockets.

Uncle Moses looked over them without ever cracking a smile, for it was a grave business. He wiped his spectacles, to examine the whole assortment.

"Here, examine them—calicoes, ribbons, laces, &c. all as good as new—no mistake—I'll take ten dollars in *coon skins* for the whole invoice, which is less than cost, rather than *tote* them any longer."

Uncle Moses was, in truth, a trading character. He belonged to a numerous and respectable class in our country, who are, by courtesy, called farmers; but who, in fact, spend their whole lives in buying and selling. He was *raised* in North Carolina, and had regularly emigrated westwardly, once in every three or four years, until he had passed through Tennessee, Kentucky, and Illinois, to the frontier of Missouri. Nothing ever made him so happy as an offer to buy his farm. The worthy man would snap his fingers, ask a little more than was offered, and at last take what he could get, pack up his moveables at an hour's notice, and push out further back. He was a famous hand at finding good land; and was sure to get a mill-seat, a stone quarry, or a fine spring, which made his tract the best in the country, and himself the happiest man in the world. He worked hard and made good improvements; but no sooner was his cabin built, his fences made, and his family comfortably settled, than he was sure to find that the neighbours were getting too thick around him, the *outlet* for his cattle was circumscribed, and there was a better country somewhere else. He was not a discontented man—far from it. There never was a better tempered old soul than uncle Moses. But he liked money, loved to be moving, and, above all things, gloried in "a good trade." He would buy any thing that was offered *cheap*, and sell any thing for which he could get the value. He never travelled without exchanging his horse, nor visited a neighbour without proposing a speculation.

Of course, the Major's offer of a lot of *store goods*, for less than cost, struck him favourably, and he offered three dozen racoon skins for the whole. "Take them," said the Major—"it is too little—but if Wan does'nt like the trade, I'll pay the balance myself."

"Now," said the postmaster, "let us go down to the river, where Hunt, and *the balance of the boys*, are fishing. We have been holding an election here for the last two days, and as nobody came in to vote to-day, we all concluded to go fishing."

"But what election is it?"

"Why, to elect delegates to form our state constitution."

"I have heard of it, but had forgot it. I am entitled to a vote."

"Certainly you are. Hunt and I are two of the judges. He has taken the poll-books along with him—come along, we will take your vote at the river—just as good as if it was done in town—I hate formalities, and this three days' election—every body could as well do all their voting in one."

Down they went to the river; the judges and clerks were called together, and recorded the first vote that ever uncle Moses gave in Missouri, on the bank of *North river,* a little below where Massie's mill now stands. I like to be particular about matters of importance.

The parties were soon distributed in quietness along the shore, angling for the finny tribe, which sported, unconscious of danger, in the limpid element. Every tongue was silent, and all eyes resting on the lines, when Sam Smoke made his appearance, cracking his way through the bushes. "Mose! come this way," said he. Uncle Moses, discovering something momentous in his air, met him at a respectful distance. "Now, Moses," said the odd old genius, "I know, very well, you have some notion of *entering** Wolf Harbour. I have *located* that place myself long ago; but I don't believe you know it. I will now let you into a secret that you have been some time hunting for, if you will not enter the land about Wolf Harbour before I get my money from Kentucky. The quarter section, including the big spring, is all I want—the balance is not worth entering—and if I can get that, I shall have all the elbow room I want."

"But what is the secret?" said uncle Moses, anxiously.

"You have been hunting for a silver mine—hav'n't you?"

"I have; do you know where it is?"

"No, I do not; but I have left an Indian in a *swing* that I have just completed for the major's amusement. He will swing himself until my return. He has a piece of the ore, and will show us the place where he found it, for a gallon of whiskey. Now, say I shall have Wolf Harbour, and you may have the silver mine."

"Agreed," said uncle Moses, "and for fear somebody else should take a fancy to it, if you will go home with me, I will loan you the money to pay for it."

---

*Buying from the government.

"No, I am much obliged to you," said Sam, "all I want, is the *chance*, after my money comes."

Uncle Moses found the Indian, as was expected, and took him home with him, where he found his cousin David, just arrived from Kentucky. "Ah! Davy, my boy, I am glad to see you. I have found, or rather I am about to find, the silver mine that I wrote to you about. See here! this is as pure silver ore as ever was seen. This yellow fellow knows where it is, and is to show it to me in the morning."

"That's very well, " said David, "but do you know you will find this fellow here in the morning?"

"No doubt of it. I know too much of the Indian not to know how to manage him. I will give him a taste out of that keg, and let him understand that there is more, and you could not whip him away."

Early the next morning, our miners had every thing ready for the expedition. The best horse was packed with the tools, and provisions enough for several days. The Indian guide was directed to lead the way. He hesitated for a moment, as if deliberating upon the course, and then, having fixed it in his mind, set off on a *bee line* towards the hidden treasure. Uncle Moses and David led the pack-horse, and plodded on foot at a half trot; for that is the gait of an Indian, when he has a journey before him. After about two hours' rough travelling through the woods and thickets, the miners were saluted with an "Ah! ho! ah!" from the Indian, who had stopped on the side of a hill a little in advance. "Plentee bel-le good·chomac," said he, holding up a piece of the precious ore, glistening in his hand. "By the wars, Davy," exclaimed uncle Moses, as he walked up and surveyed the spot, "this is a pretty good prospect—this looks well, to be sure—a right smart chance of metal, I declare!"

The horse was soon unpacked, coats off, and every thing ready for deeper research. Davy took the pick and shovel, and commenced removing the ground which seemed to cover the vein. Uncle Moses sauntered about to examine the line trees, and discover the number of the section; and the guide, having fulfilled his part of the bargain, was left in full possession of the jug, and in a few minutes, was as happy as if he had millions in store.

Uncle Moses returned in a short time, having traced the lines of the tract, and found David as wet with sweat, as if he had been in the river. "Stop, David," said uncle Moses, "you will kill yourself if you go on at this rate—give me the shovel, and rest awhile—you have blistered your hands already." This was literally true, and is usually the case with the first essay in mining; the fascination is so great, that the young miner, continually imagining himself almost in sight of boundless wealth, delves on harder and harder, and exhausts his strength, while his hopes yet remain fresh. Uncle Moses proceeded more systematically, and, in about two hours, uncovered the bright vein. What a glorious sight met their eyes! How were their hearts gladdened by the brilliant success of their enterprise! They paused, and silently contemplated the shining mass, which lay in a perpendicular stratum, several inches in thickness, and extended along the whole length of the opening. Again they resumed their labours, traced the vein into the side of the hill, and satisfied themselves, that, according to uncle Moses' estimate—and he was not slow at a calculation—there was, at least, fifty thousand dollars' worth of pure silver then within their grasp. "That is enough to make us both rich," said David.

"Why, it is better than nothing," replied the old speculator, gravely, and with all the importance of one who felt the inward dignity of a nabob; "yes, it is better than making corn, or trading in store goods—fifty thousand dollars is a clever little sum. But it is nothing to what is coming—nothing to the balance that lies in the bowels of the earth."

Having rested a little from their labour, the dinner-bag was produced, and they sat down to a cold luncheon, which Davy pronounced to be the sweetest morsel he ever ate in his life. "I don't doubt it," replied uncle Moses; "this is one of the real enjoyments of this world. And now, David, since I have made your fortune, I hope you may so manage it as never to lose your relish for the substantials, by indulging too much in the luxuries of life."

"Never fear that," said David; "I have been raised to industry—I intend to go to the legislature. It takes less head than any thing else that I know of, and I never heard of a member losing his appetite for meat or liquor. But who have we here?"

"If it aint that old Hibbard and his hungry gang of tall boys," exclaimed uncle Moses; "he has been hunting for this very mine for several months. They have been watching us—they have a canoe at the river, and will try to be at St. Louis first to *enter* the land. You are a light rider, Davy, and there is my horse—I gave a hundred and fifty dollars for him—better stuff was never wrapped in a surcingle—fix the saddle, mount him, and put off."

Davy was soon ready. Uncle Moses slipped a roll of bank notes in his hand, and the junior partner in the silver mine wrapped them carefully in a handkerchief, which he bound round his body—conducting the whole operation with an apparent carelessness, to deceive those who were looking on.

"There is the money," whispered uncle Moses, "and two hundred dollars over, to buy horses if needful. Ride slowly off, as if you were going home, and when out of sight take a *dead aim* for St. Louis. Don't lose any time looking for roads—a road is of no account, no how, when a man is in a hurry. Don't spare horse flesh. We can afford to use up a few nags in securing a silver mine. If any body asks your business, you know what to say—it's nothing to nobody. Buy the land before you sleep. I'll camp here till you return, and keep these wolves off."

David obeyed orders, and was soon on a high prairie of parallel ridges extending southward. He involuntarily stopped and gazed with wonder and delight on the first specimen which his optics had ever beheld, on so large a scale, of Nature's meadows. He was naturally of a sanguine temperament and lively imagination, and enjoyed the scene with a higher relish, from its sudden and unexpected appearance. "It beats all," thought he; "I'd give a thousand dollars, (an hour before he would have said *a dollar,*) to know who cleared up all this land. The day has been, when thousands of acres of tobacco have been raised on these *old fields*—but who raised it? When I get the silver mine I'll find it out. Yes, I'll hire a half a dozen Yankee schoolmasters by the job, and pay them in *pigs* of cast silver." The importance of his journey, however, soon compelled him to collect his scattered wits, and exert them in determining his course. His geographical knowledge of this country was very limited, as he had passed up the Mississippi in a keel boat, and knew nothing of the interior. But he was aware that his course ought to be nearly south, and that, as the country was thinly settled, he would in all probability have to pass most of the distance without a road or trace of any kind.

He followed the direction of one of the ridges of the prairie, and travelled rapidly, until his progress was suddenly arrested by a deep stream, about a hundred yards in width, margined on each side with a heavy growth of tall timber. "This must be Salt River," said he. It was too deep to ford, and the only alternative was to swim—a feat he would sooner have attempted at some place where assitance might be had in case of accident. But knowing that the defeat of his enterprise, and certain loss of his expected wealth, awaited him if he did not cross, he screwed up his resolution, and determined to pass or drown in the attempt. His money was placed in his hat, and he plunged in; his horse was of powerful muscle, and bore him safely to the opposite shore.

The sun was gilding the west as he emerged into another beautiful prairie, carpeted with the matchless verdure of the season, which extended further than his vision could reach. The evening was calm and pleasant; a soft breeze only moving to fan the sweet perfume of the various flowers which spotted the plain. Not a cloud was to be seen. The lark, whistling on the rosin-weed, or a solitary hawk, circling through the air, now poised aloft, and now darting, with the swiftness of an arrow, on the half concealed sparrow below, were the only moving objects on which to rest the eye of the traveller. The scene was solitary as it was grand, and naturally led our weary adventurer into a contemplative mood. He thought of the many instances he had known of the misapplication of the gifts of fortune, and determined, in his own mind, as he was now heir, apparently, to a princely estate, that he would use it in such a manner as to afford the most solid advantages to himself and his country. He resolved to found schools for the education of all classes, to make roads, and to build bridges—especially one over Salt River. He had a mortal antipathy to the aristocracy of wealth, and vowed that he would level the rich down to an equality with the poor; or, if that should be impracticable, he would level the poor *up* to the standing of the rich. His fondness for the fair sex induced him to wish to confer happiness on as many of them as possible; but as it was impracticable, under the present organization of society, to confer supreme bliss on more than *one*, he determined to make one happy woman, at least, without delay.

At length, night began to drop her curtain around him, and to stud the skies with her twinkling lamps. The dew rested on the tall grass, and, as the tops of the latter were sometimes higher than his horse's back, his own clothes soon dripped large drops of water. Still he pushed on, until the weary animal, by often stopping to nip the green herbage, admonished him that food and rest are necessary to brute creatures, however non-essential they may be to the proprietors of silver mines. But it was not until drowsiness had so overpowered him that he was several times on the point of losing his balance, that he determined to rest for the night. He then dismounted, tied his horse's feet together with the reins of the bridle, supped on some cold venison and corn bread, that uncle Moses had put into his saddlebags, and crawling into a matted hazel thicket, nestled among the leaves, and slept soundly until morning.

With the first blush of the dawn, David was again on his way, somewhat refreshed. But the wolves having robbed his saddlebags of the remaining provisions, he had nothing wherewith to break his fast. He jogged on at a pretty rapid gait, however, fully determined to compensate his appetite hereafter, in the most ample manner, for the privation it was now suffering. "Poor devils, that have neither house nor land," said he, "may travel upon empty stomachs, and *camp out* in the bushes at night, but that will not be my case. I intend to have old bacon all the year round; and let them eat venison who can get nothing better."

About the middle of the afternoon, he stopped at the first cabin he had seen, and enquired of a homespun lady, who appeared at the door, if he could get something for himself and horse to eat. After asking him a dozen questions about "where he was from—where he was going—how the election had gone—whether he thought the *convention* would make this a free or slave state—where he staid last night—and if he *war'nt mighty* tired?"—she at last told him "to light." She soon had every thing ready, and invited him to "set up" and help himself, remarking "that it was not very good fare, no how, but if she had known of his coming, she would have had something better."

From this place, he found a road leading to St. Charles, where he expected to cross the Missouri. Sleepy and weary, every rod seemed now a mile, and he had not gone far from the cabin, when he stopped a traveller, that he met, to enquire the distance to St. Charles; "thirty miles," was the reply.

After proceeding a half a mile further, he fell in with another, who told him it was "fifteen miles"—a boy, to whom he put the same question, replied that "it was a *good little bit*"—and a farmer, a little further on, informed him that the exact distance was "twenty-one miles from the big oak at the foot of his lane."

It was dark, when he concluded, for the last time, that he must certainly be within a short distance of the river; and, at length, meeting a negro on the brink of a hill, was assured that it was "not no distance at all." He was soon in the village of St. Charles, and had no difficulty

The Silver Mine.

in finding the ferryman, who refused, positively, to carry him across the river that night. David had too much at stake to be thus delayed. He stormed—threatened to cut off the ears of the boatman—swore he would kick the mud-walled house from over the head of the unaccommodating Frenchman—and, finally, talked about regulating the whole town.

"Monsieur Kentuck," said the ferryman, "vat make you so dem hangry? are you in von great big horry?"

"I am on business of importance—more depends on it than your paltry gumbo town is worth—so, stir yourself, or I'll be shot if I don't make a fuss."

"Very much horry, eh?" replied the Frenchman—a dark, swarthy fellow, with straight, black hair, and an eye which began to flash with an *amiable* expression, resembling that of an enraged wild-cat. "'Spose den you vait for your horry over—mean time, you cut off *ma hear* for keep yourself warm!"

Davy, finding he was on the wrong scent, changed his tone, said he had no wish to affront *any gentleman,* and enquired, in a soothing tone, *if money* could procure him a passage.

"Ah, Monsieur, now you talk like von gentiman—'spose you pay me five dollar, may be you cross de Missouri—'spose you no pay me dat, you may go sleep on dis side, sacre!"

Davy accepted the terms: the *ferry boat,* consisting of two canoes covered with a platform, was hauled up, the horse carefully placed in the middle, and the *savage river,* which roared and bubbled around them, was soon passed. The ferryman pointed out the road, and in a few hours our impatient Kentuckian was at the door of the receiver of public monies in St. Louis, shouting manfully, "Who keeps house?" Colonel S., the receiver, from an upper window, told him that he could not *enter* the land, nor the land office, that night; it was positively contrary to all rule—and Davy, much chagrined, was obliged to sneak off to a hotel. In the morning he hied by times to the land office, and found, to his mortification, that the whole section was covered by a New Madrid claim! Excited now to desperation, he declared that he would work the silver mine, *any how,* in spite of big guns and little men—he did'nt *vally* the government a cent—not he—it was *no account, no how*—then he jumped up, struck his heels together, and said he was a horse, a steam-boat, an earthquake—and that he and uncle Mose, with a hundred Kentuckians, could take Gibraltar!

Hanging his hat on one side of his head, he strutted out of the office, endeavouring to control his rage, and half inclined to gratify it, by whipping the first man he should meet. Finally, however, he concluded to send an express to uncle Moses, and set out for Kentucky himself, to raise volunteers enough to set the land officers at defiance, nullify the government, and work the silver mine, *vi et armis*. Meeting with Mons. Donja, an old acquaintance who was a silversmith, he exultingly produced a specimen of the precious ore, and asked his opinion of it.

"Vat you call dis?" said the dealer in bright metals.

"Pure silver ore—the real stuff."

"You mistake, sair; dat is no silvare, but be ver good brimstone!"

"Brimstone, the devil!" shouted the enraged adventurer.

"Ah, oui," replied the mechanic, with a shrug, "very good brimstone for diable; suppose you go in my shop, you shall be satisfy."

Davy went, and was soon convinced, by being almost suffocated with the fumes of sulphur.

This was the climax of disappointment; but David was blessed with a sanguine temperament, and, although easily irritated, had the faculty of as easily abandoning a favourite scheme, in favour of some new project; and, after giving a long whistle, he strolled back to the hotel with an air of so much unconcern, that no one would have dreamed that any sinister event had befallen him. "It all comes of trusting too much to uncle Mose," thought he; "the old man used to be as true on the scent of money as an old 'coon dog on a pest trail—but he is barking up the wrong tree this time."

He now ordered his horse. "Sorry to inform you," replied the landlord, "very sorry, sir—but, your horse is dead."

"Dead!"

"Dead as a house log."

"Misfortunes never come single," said David; and quietly throwing his saddle over his shoulder, he walked off, singing, from Hudibras or some other celebrated poet,

> "He that's rich may ride astraddle,
> But he that's poor must tote his saddle."

THE SEVENTH SON.

I had a classmate at college whose name was Jeremy Geode. Circumstances threw us together at that time, and we became attached friends. We occupied the same room and the same bed, and freely communicated to each other our most secret thoughts. I am not philosopher enough to account for the principle of attraction which operated upon us; the adhesion was very strong, but the cause that produced it was as deeply hidden from my feeble power of perception as the properties of the loadstone. I once read a very learned and unintelligible book of philosophy, from beginning to end, for the purpose of finding out why it was that two human beings should be stuck together like particles of granite: but I had my labour for my pains. The reason was inscrutable; stuck together we were, and yet never were two individuals more unlike each other. We were perfect antipodes, and our friendship a moral antithesis. My readers will enter fully into the perplexities which this subject afforded me, when I inform them that my friend was dismally ugly, while I was not only a great admirer of beauty, but in my own opinion, at least, very good-looking. He was a sloven, I was neat and dressy. He loved books, I loved men—particularly those of the feminine gender. He was devoted to figures, and so was I—but then his affections settled upon the figures of arithmetic and geometry, while mine were running riot among those of the cotillion. He was studious, grave, and unsocial, and I gay, volatile, and fond of company. I could talk by the hour about any thing, or about nothing, while my friend was taciturn, seldom opening his remarkably homely mouth except to utter a syllogism or demonstrate a problem. There were occasions, it is true, when his eloquence would burst forth like the eruption of a volcano. I have seen him rant like a stump orator over a geological specimen, or pour forth metaphors in all the exuberance of poetic phrensy, while commenting upon the wonders exhibited in the structure of a poor, unfortunate mosquito which had fallen into his clutches. Strange as it may seem to those who are unacquainted with the organization of such minds, he was a wit of the highest order. A sly inuendo, a sententious remark, a playful sarcasm, uttered with the most inflexible gravity, would excite in others a paroxysm of laughter, while he was apparently unconscious of any feeling akin to mirth. That he enjoyed his own exquisite vein of humour and the humour of others, I have now no doubt, for every man who possesses any strongly-marked faculty of the mind experiences a high degree of pleasure in its exercise. But he passed for a misanthrope, an unfeeling, selfish man, who, wrapped up in the abstraction of his own mind, had no sympathies in common with his fellow-creatures; and he was willing to pass under any character which might secure him from intrusion, and leave him at liberty to pursue the leadings of his own genius. His equanimity under these surmises, and under all the crosses of life, was absolutely miraculous; the truth was, that his vigorous understanding and native good temper enabled him to look down upon the accidents that vex other men. I alone suspected that he was kind and generous, because I had seen his eye moisten and the rigid muscles of his face relax as he perused the tender epistles of a doating mother; though it was only in after years that I learned that he earned his own subsistence and that of his parent by the labours of his pen, while he pursued his college studies. I could have wept when this fact came to my knowledge, and when I recollected how I had sometimes ridiculed his parsimonious habits and his unceasing devotion to labour.

Another trait in the character of my friend shall be chiefly noticed. Although he diligently eschewed the company of women, and regarded men with careless indifference, he seemed so perfectly enamoured of the society of children and other irrational animals, that I sometimes suspected him of being a believer in the Pythagorean doctrine of transmigration. When fatigued with mental exertions, he would steal off to join his little playfellows on the green beyond the town, which was their place of evening resort. There he would be seen stretched upon the grass, gazing at them with an eye of interest and of complete satisfaction. The youngsters quickly struck up an acquaintance, and cleaved to him with instinctive affection. They soon learned to bring him their hats and coats to take care of when they drew them off for play; he became the umpire in their contests and the peacemaker in their disputes; and he might often be seen with the whole *posse* around him, the smallest hanging on his knees and his great shoulders, and the biggest forming a dense circle, with open eyes and mouths, while he related some strange legend or explained the curious phenomena of nature. These facts were not generally known in college; and it was well for him—for had the erudite and dignified Sophomores detected him in such childish pursuits, my friend Jeremy Geode would undoubtedly have been put in Coventry. He had a mocking-bird, too, in a cage, a martin-box at his window, and an industrious family of silk-worms in a small cabinet. A lean, hungry, ferocious-looking cat, whose love of mice or of mythology had brought her to college, who had been expelled from one room, and kicked out of another, and suffered martyrdom in so many shapes, that, but for the plurality of her lives, she would long since have ceased to exist, at last took refuge in our room. She entered with a truly feline stealth of tread, and sought concealment with the cowardice of conscious felony. But no sooner did she attract the eye of Jeremy, than a mutual attachment commenced, a single glance revealed to each a kindred spirit; in a few hours puss was running between the student's feet; before the close of the day she was reposing in his lap, and a firm friendship was cemented. Under his care she grew fat, social, and contented, and justice requires me to say, that a more intelligent or better behaved cat never inhabited the walls of a learned institution.

After the completion of our college course, we commenced the study of our respective professions. Now it was that a principle of repulsion began to operate, which carried us perpetually in opposite directions. Our minds, which had heretofore, to some extent, inhabited the same sphere, began to diverge, as it were, from a common centre, so that we entered upon the great theatre of life by different paths. My friend, who was cautious and plodding, betook him to the dusty turnpike of science, carefully noting the indications of the innumerable finger-posts and mile-stones, which have been set up by the industry of sundry worthy men on either side of that great highway. He was willing to reach the ultimate point of his ambition by the beaten road, which experience had marked out. Wisdom's ways are said to be pleasant ways, and all her paths peace, and I dare say he found them so; but I must confess that I had not sufficient taste to discern wherein that peace and pleasantness consisted. I betook myself to that flowery path, which, without having any particular source or destination, meanders through the regions of fancy and the resorts of pleasure. But I was unwilling, at first, to part with my friend; I grieved to see his youth withering in monastic seclusion, and his energies wasted in a severe course of unproductive studies.

"What do you expect to gain," said I to him, one day, "by this incessant toil of the mind, this rigid self-denial, this total abstraction from the ordinary pursuits of youth?"

"Knowledge!" was his laconic reply.

"And will the accumulated stores of knowledge be worth so dear a purchase? Are you not acting the part of the miser who keeps up a mass of useless wealth, at the expense of all the courtesies of life, and all its enjoyments? Is this a rational way of spending time?"

"I like it," said he.

I was nettled at his perfect composure. "So does your cat like sleep," I exclaimed, "and pardon me for saying that I see little difference"—I was going to say, "between you and your cat," but I had the grace to modify the comparison—"between dozing over the fire, or over musty books."

"The books are far from musty," replied he very placidly, "and as for poor puss, she is quite happy and respectable, in her way."

"But, my dear Geode, to what end is this slavery of mind?"

"Usefulness."

"Usefulness? to whom, pray?"

"To myself, to my country, to mankind."

"And the reward? Come, tell us that. What do you expect in return for becoming the benefactor of an ungrateful world?"

"The approbation of good men and of my own conscience."

He had reason and virtue on his side, and my logic would hold out no longer. I was awed, but not convinced; and we parted.

My friend studied medicine, a choice upon which I had often rallied him as growing out of his love for the occult sciences; for with his more solid acquirements he had mingled an acquaintance with alchemy, witchcraft, and all the mystic lore which is found in black-letter books. He could draw horoscopes and tell fortunes like an adept, and so gravely would he talk upon such subjects, that had it not been for a lurking roguishness of the eye, which he could never wholly command, I should have feared that he was in earnest. I chose the science of law, because this profession is considered the path to office and honour. I had no relish for the drudgery of a practising attorney. Framing declarations and exploring the intricacies of law reports had no attractions for me. My ambition soared higher; and I imagined, as multitudes of young men do, who crowd to the bar in the hope of leading a life of ease and dignity, that my labours would cease, and my triumphs begin, with my maiden speech. In common with all who have been deluded by this fallacy, I have discovered my error. The labours of the lawyer who pursues his profession with energy are as severe as those of the farmer or mechanic, while his pecuniary gains are less certain. But then the farmer is a drudge and the mechanic is not an *esquire.* The legal profession confers a patent of gentility on its members; they are *gentlemen* of the bar; and the man who wishes to become a gentleman by a short cut, and to remain one during life, has only to procure a license to practise in a court of record, which confers an indefeasible title to that distinction, whatever may be the properties of his body, mind, or estate.

But I sat down, not to write of myself, but to indite the veritable history of Doctor Jeremy Geode, who, having obtained his diploma with great distinction, emigrated to the Western States. He called to take leave of me, previous to his departure. A suit of mourning announced that he had lost his mother, the only human being in memory of whom he would have thought it necessary to exhibit this outward symbol of grief. "I nursed her," said he, "in her last illness, and received her blessing. It was mournful to sever so dear a tie; but I felt that I had gained, in her approbation of my conduct, a richer legacy than any that the whole earth could bestow." He spoke of his future prospects with confidence, though with that peculiar bashfulness with which a modest young man, accustomed to seclusion, faces the world for the first time. There is no sight more touching to a considerate heart, than to behold a highly gifted and ingenuous youth embarking in the voyage of life with no companion but enterprise and indigence. Bright may be his career and noble his triumphs, but the chances that those buoyant hopes, those modest graces, those virtuous emotions, which render youth so engaging, will be blighted by vice, by disappointment, and by sordid cares, are so many, as to fill the benevolent heart with trembling apprehension.

Doctor Geode settled in an obscure town, far in the wilderness. It was a village newly laid out upon the borders of an extensive prairie; a beautifully undulating plain, fringed with wood, and dotted with picturesque clumps and groves of trees. The grass, as yet but little trodden, exhibited its pristine luxuriance, and a variety of gorgeous flowers enlivened the scene. The deer still loitered here, as if unwilling to resign their ancient pastures, and at night the long howl of the wolf could be heard, mingled with the fearful screechings of the owl. The village was composed of log-cabins, and was, with the neighbourhood around it, inhabited chiefly by backwoodsmen—a race of people, who, delighting in the chase, and devoted to their wild, free, and independent habits, precede the advance of the denser population, and keep ever on the outskirts of society. Ardent, hospitable, and uncultivated, the stranger is as much delighted with the cordial welcome he finds at their firesides, as he is struck with their primitive manners, their singular phraseology, and their original modes of thinking. Accustomed to long journeys, to frequent changes of residence, to protracted hunting expeditions, to swimming rivers, and encamping in the woods, they bear fatigue and exposure with the patience of the Indian: their figures of speech are numerous, and drawn from natural objects; and they have a fund of that intelligence which arises from extensive wanderings, from a close observance of nature, and from habits of free discussion, mingled with the simplicity induced by the absence of literature.

A few months passed away delightfully with Doctor Geode. He roamed the forests and the prairies with the eagerness of one who had fallen upon a new world, more beautiful than that of his nativity. He walked and rode, hunted and fished, not for sport, but in search of scientific truth. The cabin which he occupied as a study soon grew into a museum of natural curiosities. Every day brought some novel and interesting subject under his investigation. The treasures of knowledge which he had accumulated over the midnight lamp, seemed now to swell and burst forth into life, as the exuberant flower springs from the folds of the bud. The world around him was teeming with living and beautiful illustrations of those abstruse principles that had been gathered into his memory with so much toil and arranged with so much care. Not a wind blew nor a shower fell, not a flower regaled his senses with its gaudy beauties or rich perfumes, without filling his mind with a sensation of pleasurable emotion. To him the phenomena of nature were all eloquence and music and symmetry. He had studied these things in the closet as mere abstractions, but now they came before him as sensible objects, bearing the stamp of reality, and glowing with the freshness and beauty of life.

But in the midst of these pursuits, my worthy friend entirely forgot to employ the ordinary means of getting into practice. He made no display of his skill nor courted the acquaintance of any of his neighbours. No flashy advertisement extolled the merits of Doctor Geode and informed the public that he was their humble servant. A wily competitor, taking advantage of this improvidence, represented my erudite friend as an insane gentleman, who roamed about gathering roots and catching prairie flies, and the neighbours felt no inclination to consult a mad doctor. His own habits confirmed these mercenary slanders. His homely face was pale and sallow; his thick black beard was often allowed to remain a whole week unshaven; and in his total carelessness of every thing relating to his own comfort, he sometimes walked from his shop to his lodgings without his hat, or with one boot and one shoe. His collection of stuffed birds, impaled insects, and pickled reptiles might well bring his sanity in question with those who could see no advantage in this hideous resurrection of dead bodies. Moreover, he had tamed a crow, a bird held in particular aversion, in consequence of its depredations upon the corn-fields, and pronounced by a popular verse to have been,

> "Ever since the world began,
> Natural enemy of man;"

and a black cat, who of her own accord had taken up her residence with him, was his constant companion. He soon found himself avoided, like a mad dog in a populous town, or a freemason in the enlightened State of New York. Week after week rolled away, and not a patient called the skill of Doctor Geode into requisition. He wondered at this circumstance, and perplexed himself with vain endeavours to conjecture the reason. He saw that he was even shunned, but his modesty as well as his independence prevented him from inquiring into the cause. In the mean while his finances were exhausted, and poverty, with all its inconveniences and mortifications, stared him in the face.

There is one truth, as regards the moral government of this world, to which there are few exceptions; it is that good deeds always have their reward. So it happened to my friend. He was one day induced to enter a solitary cabin, in the outskirts of the village, by hearing, as he passed, the groans of a person who seemed to be in pain. A decent widow, who supported a large family by her labour, was suffering under a high fever and in a state of delirium. Beside her sat a fair-haired girl, about fourteen years old, the daughter of a neighbouring gentleman, bathing her temples and vainly endeavouring to soothe her torture. Without asking any questions, the humane physician rendered such assistance to the sufferer as her case required; nor did he quit her bedside till every alarming symptom was removed. The young girl; who at first shrunk back in alarm, was soon drawn to his assistance by the kindness of his tones, and now witnessed his promptitude and success with astonishment. He continued to attend from day to day until his patient was completely restored, and then refused any compensation for what he considered a slight and a voluntary service. Being an intelligent woman, who had been accustomed to attend the sick, she readily discovered, from his tender manner and skilful prescriptions, that he was no ordinary man; and she now, in the warmth of her gratitude, revealed to him the arts by which his competitor had deprived him of the confidence of the public.

Doctor Geode never did things like other men. Instead of getting angry, he was amused at the ingenuity of his rival, and at his own ridiculous predicament. He was born *too far east* to be overreached by a specious pretender; and as his necessities were at that moment particularly pressing, he soon devised a plan for present relief, and for the utter discomfiture of his rival. Although his bashfulness and habits of abstraction had kept him aloof from an intercourse with his neighbours, he had not been inattentive to their traditions and modes of thinking; while he spoke little, he had listened and observed much. Some of their superstitions had struck him as remarkably amusing, and he was even then preparing an essay on this subject. With these landmarks to assist him, his scheme was soon digested. Having prepared a neat card, and drawn upon it a circle and a triangle with red ink, he proceeded to trace over it several words in the Greek character. He then advertised that "Doctor Jeremy Geode, the seventh son of a celebrated Indian doctor, would cure all diseases, by means of the wonderful Hygeian Tablet, or Kickapoo Panacea, of which he was sole proprietor." It was a happy thought! the virtues of a *seventh son* have long been well known; and however our sturdy borderers may dislike their savage neighbours, the *Indian doctor* has always been in high repute among them.

The reputed lunatic was at once elevated into an inspired mediciner; the crow, the black cat, and the collection of natural curiosities became objects of respectful curiosity. In vain did the *regular* physician of the village denounce him as an imposter; in vain an incredulous few professed their entire disbelief. The doors of the seventh son were soon crowded with the halt and the sick. Among the first that came was Mr. Jones, the father of the fair-haired girl, a gentleman of information and property; a frank, hospitable man, who had taken up a favourable opinion of the doctor, and who became now, by his daughter's account of the incident she had witnessed, warmly engaged in his interest. What passed at the interview need not be repeated: Mr. Jones at its conclusion exhibited evident symptoms of having enjoyed a hearty laugh, and Doctor Geode had received some new views of Western character. They remained firm friends, and Mr. Jones never spoke of the seventh son but in terms of high respect.

The success of the mystic tablet was triumphant, and its fame spread far and near. Nauseating and dangerous drugs were decried as useless and pernicious. It even became a matter of general remark and wonder, that people should be so stupid as to swallow deadly poisons, while health could be so much more cheaply purchased by looking at a card. Faith alone was requisite to give efficacy to the spell. It is true that the charm sometimes failed; but this was always attributed to the unbelief of the patient, and the doctor forthwith proceeded to treat such cases *secundum artem*, concealing the fact that he used the subtile minerals of the pharmacopœia, and leaving the world to suppose that he practised only with the simples gathered in his botanic excursions. The consequence was that his practice spread not only through the country around, but an immense number of patients were brought to him from a distance. As for the *regular* physician, he was obliged to quit the village.

Happening to pass through that region, when the fame of Doctor Geode was at its zenith, I was astonished to hear the name of my old classmate, of whom I had lost sight for some years, coupled with miraculous cures by faith; and I determined to pay him a visit. Muffled in my cloak, and disguised still further by the alteration that time had made in my features, I entered his dwelling. It was a spacious log-house, divided into several apartments, all of which, except one, were occupied by the sick. In the audience room, if I may so call it, sat the doctor; his black beard, which he had suffered to grow, overhanging his breast, and his raven locks almost concealing his features; while his mountainous nose, his calm but piercing eye, and his sarcastic lip, revealed to me, at a glance, my former classmate. He was surrounded by a group of persons who sought relief from real or imaginary diseases.

"I have a desperate *misery* in my side," said one.

"I've got the *billiards* fever," groaned another.

"I am *powerful weak*," drawled a third.

"My limbs are *sort o'* dead like," whined a fourth.

"Oh, doctor, I've got the *yaller janders* powerful bad; I feel *jist* like I'd *naaterally* die off; and I can't *hope* myself, no how."

"Can you cure the rheumatiz?"

"I've an inward fever."

"Doctor, my *peided* cow is in a *desput bad fix* with the *holler* horn."

"Ah, Doctor Geeho, you never *seed sich* a poor afflicted *crittur* as I be, with the misery in my tooth; it seems like it would *jist* use me up *bodyaciously.*"

"Oh, doctor, doctor, I've got the shaking *ager* so mighty bad, I aint no account, no how."

"Mr. Geehead, I wish you'd look at my boy; he's got in the triflingest way you ever *seed;* he can't larn his book, and does nothing but jeest tell lies and steal, *study,* all the time; he aint in his right mind, no how."

"Canst thou minister to a mind diseased?" inquired I in a feigned tone. His quick eye, which had more than once rested on me, since I had entered the room, was turned hastily towards me in eager scrutiny. Failing to penetrate my disguise, he civilly inquired my business.

"I know," said I in a mock heroic tone, "that knowledge is thy idol, usefulness thy creed, the approbation of good men thy reward. I seek advice."

"Your complaint?" he inquired in a tremulous voice, for he more than suspected who was his visitor

"The *cacoethes scribendi.*"

"Oh, *si* sick *omnes!*" exclaimed the seventh son, waving his hand over his valetudinarian levee, who stood gasping in awe at this outlandish dialogue.

"It hath afflicted me from my youth," rejoined I.

"Get you gone," cried he in a tone of grave sarcasm, while a joyful recognition sparkled in his eye, "Get you gone, it is a loathsome, incurable disease, which criticism may correct, but the grave only can remove. It hath afflicted the world for ages, carrying with it revilings and jealousies and war. It maketh a man lean in flesh and poor in substance. A hollow eye, a sunken cheek, a soiled finger, and a tattered coat, are its symptoms."

"I crave a private consultation, learned doctor," said I, and accordingly, after dismissing his patients, he led me into his *sanctum* and embraced me with the fervour of affectionate friendship.

I remained with him that day, and we consumed nearly the whole night in conversation. After he had recounted his adventures, I inquired how he, whose moral principles I knew to be rigid, could justify himself in assuming a character which did not belong to him.

"There is less of imposture," he replied, "in the character which I have assumed than you imagine; my father was a physician, and I am his seventh son."

"But is it right to delude the ignorant, and give your sanction to an idle superstition?"

"I will not say that it is right. Nothing is right but truth and plain dealing. Yet I am not prepared to say that it is morally wrong to do good to men through the medium of their own weakness. One half of the diseases which afflict mankind are imaginary, and should be treated as such. I practise upon this rule, and have found *faith* quite as valuable as physic."

"But is it possible that you can pursue this life with satisfaction?"

"So far as there has been any deception in it, it has been irksome. But it has afforded me a fund of amusement, and has given me an insight into the human heart which I consider invaluable. I have acquired an intimate acquaintance with the peculiarities of a most original people; have seen the workings of superstition in one of its most powerful forms; and have closely studied one of the most curious incidents of the mysterious connection between mind and matter."

"Then you have some confidence in your system?"

"Oh yes: how can I help it? I have seen the sturdy hunter, who could face the painted Indian or wrestle with a hungry wolf, quailing under a fancied or unimportant disorder, and suddenly at my bidding, by a mere volition of will, resuming his vigour and returning to his manly exercises; I have seen the drooping maiden, who withering like the autumn leaf, call back her smiles and bloom, by a simple exertion of faith. I must acknowledge, however, that my plan has been extended further, and continued longer than I intended. It was embraced partly in jest, partly under the goadings of stern necessity. My success astonished me. I saw no way to retreat. I was doing good to others and enriching myself. I am now possessed of a sufficient sum to establish me wherever I please. Besides, the bubble must soon burst; ours is not a country nor an age in which delusion can live long."

I left him on the following morning. Shortly afterwards he abandoned the scene of his success, after presenting the mystic tablet to the poor widow, who had proved so valuable a friend to him in the hour of adversity, and instructing her in the real secret of its efficacy.

* * * * * * * * *

Three years had passed away since the interview just related, when one day Doctor Geode, who was now a *regular* physician of high standing, in a city not far from that of my own residence, entered my room. I was astonished at the change which a short time had wrought in his person and appearance. He was now in his thirtieth year, and had just reached the vigour of manhood. He was plainly but neatly dressed. Good living and active employment had clothed his muscles with flesh, and brought a healthy bloom to his cheek. The sharp angles of his face had become rounded, and the clouds of care were dispersed. The clownish manners of the student had given place to the deportment of a plain, intelligent gentleman. A smile of benevolence and placid contentment sat upon his features; and I thought him by no means so ugly as he had been in his youth.

"Come," said he, "will you join me in a trip to—?"

"For what purpose?"

"During my residence there, I had a friend who treated me with kindness. He had penetrated my disguise by his own sagacity, but appreciated my motives, kept my secret with inviolable honour, and promoted my influence with all his influence. I was his family physician. He is dead, and his only daughter, the fair-haired girl whom I told you of, is about to be deprived of her inheritance by a designing relative. My intimacy with the family has put me in possession of facts, which are unknown to her, but which in my opinion will establish her claim. She is a mere child, poor thing, and does not know her own rights. Come, you have the dyspepsia, I am sure; I prescribe a long journey."

Who could resist the temptation of a tour to the frontier in company with such a man? "The seventh son shall be obeyed," said I; and the next morning found us on our way. The journey was delightful. The doctor was full of anecdote and brimful of science: both of which he poured out in copious streams. His former taciturnity had given place to conversational powers of a high order. It had never been constitutional, but was the result of circumstances. His youth had been silently and diligently employed in acquiring the knowledge which now burst forth in rich exuberance; and he reminded me of the tree that in the winter stands bare, solitary, and ungraceful, but in due season bears the leaf, the blossom, and the fruit. His inquisitive mind was continually on the stretch. I was struck with his various information, his affability, and colloquial skill.

We reached the broad prairies, and the region of thinly scattered population, and having procured horses, struck into the wilderness. The wide and beaten road was changed for the path that winded over the plains or among the tangled woods. We forded the little streams, and crossed the rivers in canoes, driving our horses before us. Instead of meeting the travelling carriage, the stage, and the loaded wagon, we encountered the solitary hunter in his blanket-coat, treading along with the stealthy step of a cat and the watching glance of the wary Indian. We lodged no longer at the inn, attended by assiduous servants, but slept at the settler's cabin, and sat as equals at his board. Two more days would have brought us to —, when my friend was taken ill. The attack was severe, and he thought his own case doubtful. There was no physician in the neighbourhood, and he himself was unprovided with such medicines as were suitable to his case. The fever was raging and the pain intense. It was one of those cases in which the crisis approaches rapidly. Two days passed, and he hourly grew worse. I was almost frantic. At length the man of the house told us of an old woman, who had lately settled in the neighbourhood, who was "a desperate good doctor."

"There was a right smart chance of sickness when she came into the settlement," continued the man, "a heap of people called on her—she had abundance to do, and she flew round among the folks mighty *peart,* I tell you. The way she fixed 'em was the right way, there's no mistake in it. I wouldn't give her for naary high larnt marcury doctor I ever see, no how."

"But this is an extreme case."

"No matter," replied the hunter cheerfully—"if the man was as cold as a wagon-tire, provided there was any life in him, she's bring him to; there's no two ways about it."

My friend smiled. "Send for the woman!" I exclaimed, "she may tell us of some remedy." A boy was accordingly mounted on the fleetest steed, and soon returned with the female Æsculapius. There was nothing peculiar in her appearance, except that she wore a large black veil, which completely concealed her features. She required to be left alone with the patient, but as I insisted on being present at the interview, an exception was made in my favour. She approached the bed, felt the sufferer's pulse, and passed her hand over his forehead, while the doctor, who seemed to recognise the skilful touch of the practitioner, mechanically put out his tongue. The woman turned to me and said in a low voice, "I can do nothing for this gentleman—he is very ill, and requires a greater physician than I am."

"Do your best," exclaimed I.

"Ah, sir, I have little skill in medicine. I am but a poor weak woman; a very humble instrument in the hands of Providence. I can do nothing here. This man needs medicine."

"If you mean to say, that you do your work by a spell, I insist upon your trying it."

"Very willingly," said the woman meekly, and then raising her voice, she exclaimed, "let no one speak."

She next turned to her patient, and said, "Sick man! do you believe that I can raise you from this bed of pain?"

The doctor, who, even in the hour of extremity, seemed to retain his relish for *hocus pocus,* nodded his head, while I felt an unaccountable awe creeping over me.

"Then look upon my face," continued she in a solemn tone, throwing back her veil, and displaying in her right hand the identical table of Doctor Geode, "and look upon this tablet of health, and these mysterious figures, and charmed words, drawn upon it by the hand of the seventh son of a celebrated Indian doctor—look upon them, and believe, and be restored."

This was more than the doctor could stand. No sooner did he behold the workmanship of his own hands and the pupil of his tuition, and witness the whole acting of that curious scene, of which he had been the inventor, than he burst into an immoderate convulsion of laughter. The woman gazed in amazement, for in the altered features of her patient she did not recognise her master. I ran to him in alarm; but he continued to laugh, rolling from side to side, throwing up his long arms, and screaming as if distracted.

As soon as he was composed enough to speak, he exclaimed, "Give her a fifty-dollar note, Charles! Go, go, good woman, you have done your duty well—go now, but do not leave the house!"

"Can it be possible," continued he, as the wondering woman closed the door after her, "can it be that there are two Richmonds in the field? No, it is my own veritable spell, and my very deputy herself!" And then he laughed again, until the whole house re-echoed the sonorous peal. The big drops rolled from his forehead. "See there!" he exclaimed, "behold the work of the *faith doctor;* here we have been labouring these two days to break this obstinate fever, and to produce a perspiration, and lo! the cunning woman has wrought the desired change in a moment!" And it was exactly so; the violent muscular action, and the sudden revolution in the patient's train of thought, had produced instantaneous relief. A profuse perspiration, succeeded by a gentle slumber, relieved the most violent symptoms. When he awoke he asked for the doctress. "I knew I was safe," said he, "as soon as I saw her face. She has a lancet and a box of calomel pills in her pocket. No man need die of a bilious fever when these are near. I lost mine on the road. Send her in." It is only necessary to add, that after a few days' careful attention from the old lady, who was really an admirable nurse, he was able to resume his journey.

In consequence of this detention, we arrived at the place of our destination too late to be of any service to the daughter of Doctor Geode's former friend, in her lawsuit. The cause had been tried, and decided against her. My worthy fellow-traveller bore this disappointment with less patience than was usual with him. He took it to heart, and brooded over it. Every day he went to see the young lady, to console her, and to try to devise some means to reassert her rights.

After a few visits, the doctor began to talk, in a very dignified strain, of the moral excellence and mental acquirements of his young friend; at the close of one week he pronounced her a *natural curiosity,* and before the end of the second, he assured me solemnly that she was a *phenomenon.* He had discovered a new scientific truth, namely, that in five years a slim girl of fourteen may be metamorphosed into a full-grown lovely woman.

"Why, Charles," said he, "there is nothing in all the arcana of nature to be compared with it; the bursting of the gorgeous butterfly from its chrysalis, the expansion of a beautiful flower, nor any of the most wonderful changes in the material world cannot equal it."

"What's the matter now, doctor?"

"Matter enough, sir; matter for curious thought. Here is this little girl, who, when I saw her last, was dressed in cotton homespun, wore a sun-bonnet, and ran on errands for her father—a little slight thing, as pale as a lily and as timid as a fawn. She sat in the corner knitting while her father and I conversed, and never raised her eyes or uttered more than one syllable at a time. I used to carry young birds, flowers, and pictures to her, as I would to any other child. Now she is a woman, as beautiful as Hebe, as hospitable as was her own warm-hearted father, and as rational as an M.D. She is a remarkable specimen—"

"If she is a specimen," interrupted I, "I can easily guess her fate. She will hardly escape so industrious a collector as yourself. Take her home, doctor, and place her in your cabinet; she would be worth a thousand dried flies or pickled snakes." The doctor put on his hat and walked off. I saw that it was all over with him.

At the end of the third week of our stay, I began to grow impatient; but my friend's "phenomenon" still engaged all his thoughts; and where is the ardent lover of science who would have been willing to relinquish so interesting a subject of investigation? He was anatomising the young lady's affections with as much patience of research as he would have bestowed on the complete skeleton of a mastodon. I popped in upon them one day unexpectedly, as they stood conversing at a window, and before I was observed or had time to retire, I heard her say in a tremulous tone:

"Indeed, Doctor Geode, I hardly know what to say—it is so sudden—so—so very unexpected—so—"

"I will tell you what to say; say Yes."

The young lady covered her face, and uttered neither yes nor no.

"I see through your case," continued the determined doctor, "all that it requires is *faith*. As I used to ask my patients here, I now ask you, have you faith *in me?*"

"It requires no exertion of credulity to believe that Doctor Geode is all that is noble and excellent," and then she placed her hand in his. The lover took it respectfully, and evidently at a loss what he ought to do next, mechanically laid his finger upon her pulse as if he expected to find thoughts of love and vows of truth throbbing in the arterial system.

I suppose I laughed, for they both turned towards me.

"Ah, Charles! what, eavesdropping? well, no matter—let me introduce you to Mrs. Jeremy Geode that is to be. We shall be married to-morrow, and the next day bid adieu to the frontier."

The wedding took place accordingly; and I need scarcely inform the intelligent reader that my friend is now one of the best and happiest of husbands, and is enjoying in the meridian of life the rich harvest of prosperity and honour, which crowns a youth of virtue, industry, and self-denial.